P9-CCH-690

Dear Reader,

Life has been a whirlwind of writing and romance
for me over the past year. *Bachelor Husband*, my
fifth Temptation novel, is just the first book in
Bachelor Arms, a wonderfully exciting new series—
a series in which I had the chance to create not one,
not two, but *three* irresistible heroes.

From "Rockford" to "Moonlighting" to "Magnum,"
I've always been in love with the classic Hollywood
private investigator. Who wouldn't be attracted to a
man that lived every day on the edge? Unfortunately,
my research proved that the day-to-day work of a
private investigator can be incredibly mundane. No
car chases, no gunfights, no sultry clients with ulterior
motives. With that in mind, I felt compelled to inject a
little excitement into Tru Hallihan's dull day.

Enter radio marriage counselor Dr. Caroline Leighton,
a.k.a. Carly Lovelace. With Caroline came more
research, only this time I didn't tell the folks at the
radio station just why I was so interested in seeing the
inside of a studio—with the lights off, of course.

Next month, you'll meet Josh in *The Strong Silent Type*
and the month after that, Garrett, in *A Happily Unmarried
Man*. But for now, I hope you enjoy Tru and Caroline's
story. I'd love to hear from you. Please write.

Sincerely,

*Kate Hoffmann*

c/o Harlequin Temptation
225 Duncan Mill Road
Don Mills, Ontario  M3B 3K9
Canada

## Come live and love in L.A. with the tenants of Bachelor Arms

Bachelor Arms is a trendy apartment building with some very colorful tenants. Meet three confirmed bachelors who are determined to stay single until three very special women turn their lives upside down; college friends who reunite to plan a wedding; a cynical and sexy lawyer; a director who's renowned for his hedonistic lifestyle and many more…including one very mysterious and legendary tenant. And while everyone tries to ignore the legend, every once in a while something strange happens….

Each of these fascinating people has a tale of success or failure, love or heartbreak. But their stories don't stay a secret for long in the hallways of Bachelor Arms.

Bachelor Arms is a captivating place, home to an eclectic group of neighbors. All of them have one thing in common, though—the feeling of community that is very much a part of living at Bachelor Arms.

# BACHELOR ARMS

**BACHELOR HUSBAND**
Kate Hoffmann
February 1995

**THE STRONG SILENT TYPE**
Kate Hoffmann
March 1995

**A HAPPILY UNMARRIED MAN**
Kate Hoffmann
April 1995

**NEVER A BRIDE**
JoAnn Ross
May 1995

**FOR RICHER OR POORER**
JoAnn Ross
June 1995

**THREE GROOMS AND A BRIDE**
JoAnn Ross
July 1995

**LOVERS AND STRANGERS**
Candace Schuler
August 1995

**SEDUCED AND BETRAYED**
Candace Schuler
September 1995

**PASSION AND SCANDAL**
Candace Schuler
October 1995

**THE LADY IN THE MIRROR**
Judith Arnold
November 1995

**TIMELESS LOVE**
Judith Arnold
December 1995

# THE TENANTS OF BACHELOR ARMS

**Ken Amberson:** The odd superintendent who knows more than he admits about the legend of Bachelor Arms.

**Josh Banks:** The strong, silent type. A financial whiz who is more comfortable with numbers than with women.

**Eddie Cassidy:** Local bartender at Flynn's next door. He's looking for his big break as a screenwriter.

**Jill Foyle:** This sexy, recently divorced interior designer moved to L.A. to begin a new life.

**Tru Hallihan:** A loner P.I. who loves 'em and leaves 'em.

**Natasha Kuryan:** This elderly Russian-born femme fatale was a makeup artist to the stars of yesterday.

**Garrett McCabe:** A confirmed bachelor whose newspaper column touts the advantages of single life.

**Brenda Muir:** Young, enthusiastic would-be actress who supports herself as a waitress.

**Bobbie-Sue O'Hara:** Brenda's best friend. She works as an actress and waitress but knows that real power lies on the other side of the camera.

**Bob Robinson:** This barfly seems to live at Flynn's and has an opinion about everyone and everything.

**Theodore "Teddy" Smith:** The resident Lothario—any new female in the building puts a sparkle in his eye.

# BACHELOR HUSBAND

## KATE HOFFMANN

**Harlequin Books**

TORONTO • NEW YORK • LONDON
AMSTERDAM • PARIS • SYDNEY • HAMBURG
STOCKHOLM • ATHENS • TOKYO • MILAN
MADRID • WARSAW • BUDAPEST • AUCKLAND

For Dona Vander Schaaf Wininsky

My only best friend and my expert on the radio business

ISBN 0-373-25625-6

BACHELOR HUSBAND

"SIX-THIRTY-SEVEN P.M. Subject exits office building with female companion. Dark hair, about five-six or seven…ah, nice legs…wearing beige suit, carrying leather briefcase."

Tru Hallihan put down his hand-held tape recorder and picked up the 35 millimeter camera from the car seat, never taking his eyes off the couple. As he adjusted the telephoto lens, the pair slowly came into focus. He pushed the shutter and the auto winder whirred, popping off a series of exposures.

"And who's the bimbo du jour, Ellis?" he murmured, shifting the lens to the woman. "Whoa, hello there! We've seen you before, haven't we? It's our mystery lady, back for another appearance." He snapped off five more exposures. "What's your name, sweetheart? Are you Ellis's little indiscretion?"

Ellis Stone's face reappeared in the frame. Another Hollywood golden boy, sun-streaked hair, perfect tan, polished wardrobe. "Typical," Tru muttered. The woman turned her cheek to accept a polite kiss. The camera whirred again and Tru waited, hoping for something more incriminating. He adjusted the focus and kept the lens trained on the woman.

She wasn't at all what he had expected from a guy like Stone. Experience had taught him that most up-and-coming Hollywood producer types liked their girls young and blond, with overdeveloped chests and underdeveloped minds. This woman had a look of subtle sophistication about her. From her flawless makeup and simple hairstyle to her designer suit, this "bimbo" radiated confidence and intelligence.

"You've got class, darling," Tru murmured. "What are you doing messing around with a married man?" This was the third time he'd caught the pair together since he'd begun working on the case a week ago, and each meeting had taken place in Stone's empty office suite—after hours.

If he was just a novice P.I., he would probably have written her off as a business associate. But Tru Hallihan had tailed one too many cheating spouses and photographed more than his share of illicit after work liaisons to write anyone off as innocent.

The pair continued their sidewalk conversation, standing a respectable distance from each other. She seemed a bit nervous, glancing over her shoulder every now and then. "Come on," he whispered in irritation. "Give me something I can use."

Though the divorce business was a highly profitable aspect of his private investigations firm, it wasn't his favorite kind of case. Unfortunately, his current cash flow situation didn't allow him to be picky, so he took the work when he could get it. His office rent was a month overdue, the electricity in his apartment had been turned off last week, and his prized '57 Cadillac convertible was being held hostage for repair costs at a local garage. It wasn't that he was broke exactly. He had quite a substantial sum of money to his name. Unfortunately though, every penny of it was tied up in high risk, high yield investments. So, life had looked pretty grim until Simon Marshall had called seven days ago.

The case had been too good to pass up. Get the goods on Marshall's son-in-law, television producer Ellis Stone—catch him in the proverbial act. And if Tru could prove grounds, he'd collect twenty-thousand dollars, five times his usual rate, and get a shot at Marshall's corporate security—a monthly retainer for the simple task of providing employee security checks. This case could provide him with all the money he would need to take his business to the next level. He'd have enough to rent a better office and hire a secretary. He'd have a big name to add to his client list and a foot in the door to other more prestigious and lucrative corporate clients.

That was the upside. But there was a downside. If he found nothing, the fee was just that—nothing. And so far, after seven solid days of surveillance, he'd found just that—nothing.

He had to admire Marshall's arrogance. The guy didn't get to be a multi multimillionaire by paying for something before it was delivered. And Tru was a gambler at heart and pretty decent divorce investigator. If Ellis Stone was getting a little something on the side, Tru would prove it—sooner or later. And with that proof in hand, Marshall would rid himself of a son-in-law who was bleeding his daughter's bank account dry.

The viewfinder went empty. Tru lowered the camera and watched as the pair walked in opposite directions. For a moment, he considered tailing her, but Ellis was his target, not the mystery lady. If they *were* having an affair, he'd see her again soon enough. She crossed the street in front of him and hopped into a white BMW. He raised the camera and trained the telephoto on the back of her car, then frantically searched his pockets for a pen as she pulled out into traffic.

His hand stilled as he attempted to focus on her license plate. But the car moved too fast and she was gone before he could make out the number. He swore to himself. A quick call to his old buddy at the California Highway Patrol would have nabbed him a name and address on the mystery lady in less than an hour. All he had now was a make and model and that wasn't enough to go on.

He waited until Ellis pulled out of the parking lot, then made a U-turn and tailed him at a discreet distance. A half hour later, Stone pulled up in front of a trendy restaurant, hopped out of his car and tossed the keys to the parking valet. Tru found a spot across the street and settled in for a wait. If he'd been dressed in something other than jeans and a T-shirt, he might have considered a drink at the bar and a quick look around. But he wasn't ready to risk being seen. Not yet. He pulled a bag of potato chips and a warm cola from the back seat and enjoyed his own dinner.

After an hour without any movement and a half bag of potato chips gone, the boredom had become unbearable. Tru flipped the key in the ignition and turned on the radio. He could spare fifteen minutes of entertainment before the battery in the "company car" started to drain. Though the nondescript sedan was perfect for surveillance, as a regular means of transportation it ranked just one step above a bicycle.

He missed his Caddy. He missed household electricity and hot coffee in the morning. He missed the sight of cash in his wallet. He was thirty-five years old and he was living like a kid, barely scraping by. There had been a time when living on the edge had held an addictive appeal to him. But now he wanted something more.

"I'm too damn old for this," he muttered, punching at the buttons on the radio.

"*Good evening, Los Angeles. You're listening to KTRL, Talk Radio L.A. and this is 'Making Your Marriage Work,' with Dr. Carly Lovelace. Tonight's subject is 'Carnal Conversations.' Let's take another call. This is Alice from Pomona. You're on the air.*"

"*Dr. Lovelace, I like to talk to my husband when we're making love, but no matter what I say, all I get in response is a few grunts and groans. Am I doing something wrong?*"

Tru smiled and reached over to adjust the volume. "Not in my book, honey," he murmured. "I love it when you talk dirty to me."

"*Alice, you're not doing anything wrong. It's all a matter of left brain versus right brain. Have you ever tried to carry on a conversation with your husband while he's watching a basketball game or fixing a dripping faucet? A man's brain is specialized. The right side controls action and the left side controls talk. Unlike women, who can talk and complete a task at the same time, men usually can't operate from both sides of the brain simultaneously. They're easily distracted, especially while completing a task as complex as lovemaking. If you're looking for talk, you're probably not going to get any action. And if you're looking for action, you'd better forget about the talk. I'd suggest you discuss this concern openly with your mate. If talking doesn't distract him and it makes you feel good, don't stop. But don't expect a response either. Just enjoy yourself and keep those lines of communication open.*"

Even through the cheap car radio, the sound of the therapist's voice was compelling, deep and dusky, like whiskey laced with honey. Tru's finger rested on the tuner, but he couldn't change the station. As the conversation turned to even more intimate subjects, he leaned back and closed his eyes, then slouched down in the seat. Listening to her was like having phone sex with a Ph.D.

Intelligence had always turned him on more than a gorgeous body or a perfect face. Unfortunately, women with brains usually looked for something more than Tru was willing to give. A casual relationship and a high IQ seemed to be mutually incompatible. So he had always settled for beauty instead of brains. It was safer that way.

Caught up in Dr. Lovelace's radio dialogue, Tru nearly missed Ellis's departure. The producer left the restaurant at 8:26 p.m. Tru followed the black Benz through Beverly Hills and halfway into Bel Air, before conceding the day. Stone was headed home and it was time for Tru to head to Flynn's for his regular Tuesday night poker game with the boys. As he drove down Wilshire, he listened to Dr. Lovelace's voice, not hearing her words, but simply soaking up the mesmerizing sound.

"X-RAY VISION," Garrett McCabe said. "That way I could see through ladies' clothing."

"I'd like to fly," Eddie said. "It would save on airfare."

Tru pulled out a chair at the poker table and mumbled a quick "deal me in" as he glanced around Flynn's. The place had been named after the dashing movie star Erroll Flynn. The decor was trendy black and white, accented by dark wood and green plants. The walls were covered with movie posters from Flynn's pictures—and those of the other swinging bachelors who inhabited the nearby Bachelor Arms apartments in its early days. The bar at Flynn's was always busy, but except for two guys playing pool, they had the back room to themselves.

"What about you, Josh?" Bob Robinson asked. "What superpower would you want?"

Josh Banks glanced up from his cards and blinked at them from behind conservative wire-rimmed glasses. "What?"

"Superpower," Bob said. "Choose one."

Josh frowned. "Russia?" he replied.

"Give me a clue here," Tru said. "What's the topic for tonight?"

"Bob started it," Eddie Cassidy explained. "He said that he'd rather be Batman than Superman. And then Garrett asked if we could have any superpower we wanted, what would we want. Bob said he would want superior strength and Garrett wants X-ray vision. I'd like to fly. And Josh said he wanted Russia. I don't think he understood what we meant by superpower."

Tru, Garrett and Josh, all tenants of the Bachelor Arms apartment building next door, had met in the laundry room at the Arms. Regular Tuesday night laundry soon evolved into the Tuesday night poker game at Flynn's. Eddie Cassidy, Flynn's bartender and an aspiring screenwriter, usually joined them after taking the liquor inventory. Flynn's resident barfly, Bob Robinson, also often played.

"So which would you want, Tru?" Bob asked.

Tru considered the question carefully. "I'd want to have the ability to be invisible," Tru said.

"A useful superpower for a private investigator," Bob said.

Tru smiled and shook his head. It never ceased to amaze him the wide variety of subjects they covered on any one Tuesday night—from politics to sports, from scientific theory to superheroes. They'd once spent a whole night discussing the source and composition of household dust.

"So, how's the script doing Eddie?" Tru asked, ready to move on to more erudite topics. The question came up on a regular basis. Eddie's script had been in development hell for as long as Tru had known him. While Eddie waited for his big break, he and his wife, Kim, scrimped and saved. The baby's arrival hadn't helped matters, but they seemed to be happy.

"Don't ask. The option with Carillon Productions fell through. It's with an agent now at TLC. TLC is a little boutique agency that specializes in romantic comedies. They've changed the title twice in six months and suggested three different sets of revisions. They've had one nibble, but I haven't heard anything yet. I wish the damn thing would sell. I could sure use the cash right about now."

"Don't worry," Garrett said. "I read the last draft and it's good. It'll sell."

If Garrett McCabe said Eddie's script would sell, Tru believed him. A popular columnist with the *Los Angeles Post*, no one felt the pulse of L.A. quite like McCabe could. His column, "Boy's Night Out," explored the trendy, the trashy, and the just-plain outrageous side of Los Angeles from a strictly male point of view. "You'll have so much money," Garrett said, "you'll have to give it to Josh to handle."

Josh looked up from his cards again. "What?" His glasses had slid down the bridge of his nose and he pushed them up with his index finger. "Is it my bet?"

"Relax, Josh, we'll let you know when it's your bet," Tru said. Josh took his poker very seriously, the same way he took everything else in life. A tax accountant by trade, Josh was a genius with numbers and usually knew his odds of winning a hand before the cards had even been dealt. He managed the tax affairs of a small, but exclusive client list that read like a Fortune 500 version of Who's Who in Hollywood. And though he seemed to pay the least attention to the game, he always went home with the most money in his pockets.

"Did you guys see there's a Marilyn Monroe festival showing over at the Emporium?" Garrett said. "Twenty-four-hour-a-day Norma Jean."

"I love Marilyn Monroe," Bob replied. "She's got the sexiest voice in the history of Hollywood. A real nice set of pipes."

"You want the sexiest voice?" Garrett asked. "Katharine Hepburn. Hands down, no discussion."

"I've always preferred Audrey to Katharine," Eddie said. "What about you, Tru? Sexiest voice in the history of Hollywood."

"Carly Lovelace," Tru said without a thought. He looked up to find the group staring at him.

"You mean the radio sex therapist?" Bob asked.

"She's a relationship therapist," Eddie corrected. "A marriage counselor. My wife never misses her program."

"You know, no one knows who she really is," Garrett said, tossing two chips into the center of the table. "Her identity is the best kept secret in L.A."

"You're kidding." Tru's investigative instincts kicked back into high gear. "How could someone with her profile keep her identity a secret in a town with no secrets?"

"It takes work, but it can be done," Garrett replied. "There's speculation in the trades that she really isn't a doctor. Hell, I've even heard that she might not even be a woman."

Tru grinned and his mind wandered back to that sound. He knew a woman when he heard one. Dr. Lovelace was definitely a female, and she possessed a voice that would melt any 1-900 line.

Tru leaned back in his chair and crossed his long legs in front of him. He suddenly felt a strange compulsion to get a look at the face behind that voice. And maybe make a little money on the side for his efforts. "I'll bet you boys that I can find out who Dr. Lovelace really is," he said. "And I'll do it by next Tuesday night."

"Our resident private investigator has issued a challenge!" Garrett clapped Tru on the shoulder. "I say we take him up on his offer."

"Here, here," Bob replied before taking a long swallow of his beer.

"I'm in," Eddie said.

Josh looked up from his cards and frowned. "The odds are on our side that he'll fail. I'm in, too."

"Thanks for the vote of confidence, Josh," Tru said.

"What are the stakes?" Garrett asked.

Tru considered his options, then smiled smugly. "If I discover Dr. Lovelace's real identity, you guys agree to pay the ransom on my Caddy. The garage won't give me the car until I pay the bill. Twenty-five dollars each should cover it." Tru glanced around the table as each one gave their assent.

"And if you lose?" Josh asked.

"I won't lose," Tru said. "There isn't a person in this city that can hide from Tru Hallihan. I'll have eight-by-ten glossies for all of you by week's end."

"But if you lose?" Garrett repeated.

"All right. If I lose . . . if I lose I'll . . . I'll walk through Flynn's on a Friday night in my boxer shorts."

"I'd pay twenty-five dollars to see that," Garrett said. "Wait until I tell Brenda and Bobbie-Sue. The girls in 1-C will want to get in on this one."

"And to sweeten the deal," Tru continued. "I'll bet that I can produce the *real* Dr. Lovelace at our next poker game." Tru knew there weren't many women who could resist him when he turned on the Hallihan charm. It was a risk, but a controlled risk. If she wasn't married, he might be able to get her to accept a date with him for next Tuesday. They'd just conveniently stop by Flynn's for a drink.

"No way," Eddie said. "She'd never agree to come here. And kidnapping is against the law."

"Eddie, you're forgetting who you're talking to," Tru joked. "Since when do I worry about the law? Besides, I'm not going to kidnap her. If she comes here, she'll come of her own free will. And if I get her here, McCabe, you agree to pay my electric bill. If I don't, I'll buy the beer at our poker games for the next three months."

"Deal," Garrett said.

Tru laid down his hand. "Pair of aces." God, it would be great to have his Caddy back again. And once he got his electricity turned back on, he'd at least be able to start the day with a decent cup of coffee. Yep, thanks to Dr. Lovelace, life was about to get back to normal.

"Full house," Josh said as he gathered the pot of poker chips.

Tru watched the last of his poker stake slide over to Josh's side of the table. He reached for his wallet, but knew he'd find nothing there. He needed some quick cash. He needed to get his life back on track. He needed to catch Ellis Stone in the act. But most of all, he needed the woman behind that incredible voice.

Tru Hallihan needed Dr. Carly Lovelace.

"YOU ARE ABOUT TO EMBARK on a new and profitable venture."

Dr. Caroline Leighton arched her brow and shot a skeptical look at the woman draped across her leather couch. Aurora Starr's riotous red hair, streaked with purple, was spread over the overstuffed arm. She snapped her gum as she flipped through a deck of tarot cards.

Caroline pulled on an errant strand of her own hair and inspected it distractedly. The deep brown color and blunt shoulder-length cut seemed mundane next to Aurora's audacious hairstyle. But Caroline had little time and even less patience to fuss with her hair. She made a mental note to add "haircut" to her "to do" list, then smiled at Aurora. "You're beginning to sound like a fortune cookie."

"I knew you'd say that," she said, jangling her bracelets as she examined her deep purple nails. "I'm psychic, you know."

"So you've told me," Caroline replied. Aurora Starr rented the suite across the hall from Caroline's in a chic Beverly Hills office building. From there, she ran the country's most popular psychic hotline, employing fourteen equally eccentric psychics. They had met a year ago when Aurora had burst into Caroline's office during lunch hour with the news that she had detected some disturbing psychic energy coming through the walls. By the end of the lunch hour, Aurora had managed to learn every detail about Caroline's marriage and subsequent divorce. Since that first impromptu reading, Aurora dropped by whenever the whim struck her, usually bearing news of bad vibes or a shoe sale at I. Magnin.

Aurora rolled over on her stomach and fixed Caroline with an inquisitive stare. "What's wrong, Carly? You seem preoccupied. The aura in this room is positively grim."

"Don't call me that!" Caroline ordered. "I should never have told you about Dr. Lovelace."

"You didn't *tell* me, Caro. I felt it, don't you remember? And now I sense something else is troubling you. Tell Aurora all the juicy details."

"What?" Caroline scoffed. "You can't figure it out yourself?"

Aurora sighed dramatically and sat up. "I can't just turn it on like a kitchen faucet. Besides, I'm exhausted and I don't feel like concentrating right now. So give me a break, all right?" She flipped her hair over her shoulder and studied Caroline through unearthly lavender eyes. "Spit it out, Caro, before I lose my patience."

Caroline sank back into her chair. "All right, but I don't want you to tell a single soul what I'm telling you." She waited for Aurora's nod before continuing. "I've been discussing the possibilities of turning my radio show into a television talk show. There's a producer named Ellis Stone who runs a production company here in town and he approached me with the idea. I told him I was interested."

"Caro, that's great! Imagine, you, a television talk show host. Of course, you'll do a show on psychics."

Caroline shook her head. "We're not really doing the traditional talk show format. The show will be an hour in length and will feature just one couple. They'll each discuss their side of their marital problem individually, with the other partner in a soundproof booth. Then we'll bring them together on stage. I'll offer advice and guidance, and of course, the audience will get the opportunity to ask questions and offer opinions."

"It sounds wonderful. So why are you radiating such negative energy?"

"Stone has set up a business reception with some executives from a television distribution syndicate for this Saturday night and I'm the guest of honor."

Aurora snapped her gum again. "Sounds like oodles of fun. Gee, I wish I could come with you but I've got to clean my cat litter box." She shuddered. "Besides, men in suits give me a headache. All those negative ions and gray flannel."

"Don't worry. You won't have to fight your psychic aversion to wing tips. You're not invited."

"Thank goodness for small favors," Aurora said.

"But my husband is," Caroline said, wincing.

"Edward? I didn't think you two were on speaking terms."

"No, not Edward. Lance Lovelace. I'm talking about that devoted husband I so conveniently bring up during my show every time I need to illustrate a particularly important point. They're all looking forward to meeting such a paragon of marital fidelity."

"So tell them the truth," Aurora suggested.

"I can't. I'm supposed to offer advice on making marriages work, yet I managed to make a total wreck of my own marriage. I know there are plenty of counselors out there who are divorced and it doesn't hurt their credibility. But Ellis seems obsessed with my successful marriage and I haven't had the nerve to tell him the truth. I don't want to lose this opportunity before I get the chance to show what I could do."

"You're a wonderful counselor," Aurora said. "You've saved a lot of marriages."

"And I've got a chance to help a lot more couples with this show. I can't risk the producers finding out I've been embellishing my own personal life to suit my professional needs." She sighed. "I wish I'd never even made Lance up. But it seemed so easy, just me, alone in the studio with the microphone and all those invisible listeners out there. Nobody knew who I was. And the radio show is entertainment, so professional ethics didn't seem to apply."

"Tell them Lance is out of town on business," Aurora suggested.

"I've used that excuse three times already and Ellis keeps rescheduling," Caroline replied. "Sooner or later, I'm going to have to produce a husband or tell them the truth. I was sort of wondering if I could borrow Darrell for the evening."

Aurora laughed. "Though Darrell is a wonderful husband, he has absolutely no talent for deception. I guess the skill isn't of much use when you're married to a psychic."

"Tell me what to do, Aurora. How do I get out of this mess?"

Aurora's expression brightened. "You're asking me for my professional advice?"

Caroline nodded, not entirely certain she should encourage Aurora.

After a long moment, Aurora stood and walked over to Caroline's desk. "I sense that you are at a crossroads. You have a very complex decision confronting you. Follow your instincts."

Another fortune cookie answer. As if Aurora had read that thought, she gave Caroline a cat-who-ate-the-canary smile and turned toward the door.

"That's what you get paid five dollars a minute for?" Caroline asked.

"Don't forget, the first minute is free. And you get what you pay for. Besides, I don't exert myself for non-believers," she said as she waltzed out the door.

Caroline pulled off her glasses, crossed her arms and laid her head down on her desk. What had ever possessed her to take the radio job? She had a thriving Beverly Hills marriage counseling practice, an upscale clientele, a lovely office—everything a dedicated thirty-five-year-old professional could want.

At first she had turned the radio job down. Not usually one to be outgoing or outspoken, Caroline considered herself too reserved to make interesting talk. But they'd asked her just to give it a try, no strings attached.

To her surprise, she found that hiding in a darkened studio, behind the guise of Dr. Carly Lovelace, she became the clever, witty personality she had always wanted to be. So, she had decided to take the job. After all, there was no chance that her clients would ever guess the connection between Lovelace and Leighton, so she had been safe. Until Ellis Stone had tracked her down and made his offer.

Despite her misgivings, she found herself considering the possibilities of the television show. Though she dished radio advice in a glib and humorous way, the advice she offered was based on well-founded therapy. The radio job *was* professionally satisfying. But on television, she could reach couples all across the country who couldn't afford a two-hundred-dollar-an-hour counselor. She could help them understand the dynamics of a relationship and encourage them to work out their problems.

But she couldn't have both—a private practice and a television career. The radio hid her identity, but television would bare all. Caroline sat up and rubbed a dull ache from her temples. Maybe it would be best to forget the television deal. The possibility created more problems than she had answers for.

Her parents, both nationally recognized therapists, would be embarrassed beyond belief. Her peers would be shocked, then scornful. And her patients would surely bolt. Besides, she wasn't even sure she could handle appearing in front of a camera without dissolving into a fit of stage fright. And backing out of the deal would take care of the sticky problem of producing her heroic husband, Lance Lovelace.

Her buzzer sounded and Caroline picked up her phone. "Your one o'clock is here, Dr. Leighton," her receptionist's voice informed. "Mr. and Mrs. Dorfmann." Janine lowered her voice to a whisper. "And they're already arguing. I could hear them before they even walked into the lobby."

After a quiet acknowledgment, Caroline placed the phone back in the cradle and pulled her purse from her bottom drawer. She stared at herself in her compact mirror, tucked a strand of hair back into the loose knot at her nape, then examined her features. She maintained her professional image with a minimum of makeup, conservative designer suits, and a cool, dispassionate demeanor.

She snapped the compact shut and sighed. Funny how her demeanor disappeared as soon as the On Air sign lit up at the radio station. It was as if she became a different person, the person that she might have become if her intellectual parents hadn't suppressed her natural desire to perform and replaced it with more educational pursuits.

How would it feel to stand in front of an audience, to see herself on national television, to be recognized as she walked down the street or shopped for groceries? In a way, the concept of celebrity was exciting. Perhaps this was her chance to explore a side of herself she had suppressed too long.

She wanted this chance and she'd do anything to make it happen. She made a mental note to add "husband" to her "to do" list, right at the top.

TRU STOOD in the reception area of the luxurious office suite. The receptionist—Janine Reed, by her nameplate—smiled at him uneasily. "She'll see me," he assured her. "Just tell her Tru Hallihan is here. I'm a private investigator and I have a personal matter to discuss with her."

Janine picked up the phone and he heard the intercom buzzer sound from an office nearby. A voice—*that* voice—answered.

"There's a private detective out here, Dr. Leighton. He'd like to see you."

The voice in the office lowered to a whisper and Janine listened carefully.

"No," she replied. "He doesn't have an appointment and he won't tell me what he wants. You've got the Bartons scheduled for nine. Would you have time to see him right now or should I have him schedule another time?"

"No. I'll see him now. Send him in."

Yes, that voice! All his doubts disappeared. It was definitely Dr. Lovelace. Two days of dead-end leads, wasted time spent charming station secretaries and wasted money bribing the custodial staff. Hours waiting outside KTRL after her show, yet never seeing a soul. He had almost admitted failure until a talkative messenger boy had mentioned KTRL's sister station in Burbank. Where better to hide the station's most valuable asset? A twenty-dollar bribe to the parking lot attendant was all it took to get her license plate number.

By early this morning, he had a name—Caroline Leighton—and a home address. A quick look in the phone book gave him a business address in an exclusive office building in Beverly Hills. He hopped into the company car, determined to see her. He told himself it was because he wanted to win the bet, but he also had to admit that he wanted to meet the woman behind the voice, to see if she matched the sexy vision his mind had created.

"Dr. Leighton will see you now. Can I get you a cup of coffee or a beverage?"

He shot the receptionist a dazzling grin. "Coffee would be wonderful, Janine. Thank you."

She returned his smile flirtatiously. "Black? Or cream and sugar?"

"Black," he replied. "And bring Dr. Leighton a cup, too. I think she'll need it."

Tru strode into her office and stopped in front of her desk. She didn't look up, her attention focused on the papers scattered in front of her.

"If you've come here for information, you must know that my clients are protected by doctor-patient confidentiality," she said calmly. "And you won't get anything out of Janine, either."

"That's not what I'm here for," he said.

She pulled off her glasses and stood up, then looked directly into his eyes. He blinked once, hard, unable to believe what he saw before him. It couldn't be! But it was. He found himself staring at the lovely face of his mystery lady. The face he'd seen just a few nights ago through his telephoto lens. The woman he suspected of having an affair with Ellis Stone. His fantasy woman with the sexy voice evaporated before his eyes, replaced by Stone's bimbo du jour.

"Is there something wrong?" she asked.

"No, no," he said. "Nothing's wrong."

"Janine said you're a private investigator. Could I see some identification?"

He reached into his back pocket, withdrew his wallet and held it out to her. She stepped around her desk and plucked it from his fingers, then retreated a safe distance before opening it. After she had carefully examined his P.I. license, she looked up at him, watching him through wary eyes.

"Harry Truman Hallihan?"

"Give-'Em-Hell Harry. My grandfather's hero. My friends call me Tru."

"Would you like to tell me why you're here, Mr. Hallihan? And who sent you?"

"No one sent me. I'm here on my own. I have an important matter to discuss with you."

"Have a seat," she said, indicating the guest chairs in front of her desk. Tru sank into the soft leather and glanced around the office. Compared to his functional twelve-by-twelve space in West Hollywood, her office was a palace. One entire wall was lined with shelves holding a variety of books and expensive knickknacks, and opposite that, a wall of windows looked out on the street. Behind her desk, the wall was plastered with awards and diplomas.

"The marriage counseling business must be booming," he murmured to himself.

Janine hurried in and delivered their coffee, gracing him with an inviting smile before she left, a smile that didn't get past Dr. Leighton. Her expression tightened.

Tru took a sip of his coffee and grinned. "Great coffee," he said.

She folded her hands in front of her and fixed him with a haughty look. "You're wasting my time, Mr. Hallihan."

Tru crossed his ankles in front of him and slouched down in his chair. She really was quite pretty, even though she worked hard at subverting her sex appeal. He wondered what she'd look like with her dark hair tumbled in disarray around her face, instead of pulled back in that schoolteacher knot. "And I can tell you're the kind of lady who doesn't like to waste time. So, I'll get right to the point. I know you're Dr. Carly Lovelace."

She shifted uneasily in her chair and her glacial calm wavered slightly. For a moment he detected a soft vulnerability in her gaze. "So?" she shot back. "Maybe I am. What do you plan to do with that piece of information? If this is some kind of blackmail scheme, it's not going to work."

Tru hesitated, wondering whether the threat of blackmail just might get him what he wanted. Instead, he feigned a shocked expression. Honesty would probably be more effective with this no-nonsense woman. "Carly, what kind of guy do you think I am? I wouldn't blackmail you. I'm just settling a poker bet."

"A bet?" she cried, jumping up from her chair. "That's what this is all about? You're wasting my time over a poker bet?" She shook her head disgustedly. "Men! I swear, sometimes your irresponsibility baffles me. A stupid bet?"

Her composure had melted completely. Ice had transformed into fire. Her emerald eyes snapped with anger and the color heightened in her perfect ivory skin. He was tempted to reach out and capture all that magnificent fury in his arms, but he thought better of it. "Not stupid," he countered. "If I find out who the real Dr. Lovelace is, I get my car back."

She stalked around her desk, then leaned against the front edge and crossed her arms intractably. "Though I'd just love to know how the two are connected, I think we're through here. I'd appreciate it if you'd keep your knowledge of Dr. Lovelace to yourself. You may leave now."

"Actually, we're not through. I need a photo of you. I promised the guys I'd bring pictures." Tru reached into his pocket and pulled out a miniature camera. He held it up and snapped a picture of her. "Could you at least smile?" he asked, as he snapped another exposure.

She snatched the camera out of his hand and pried the back open, then yanked the film out. Tossing it back at him, she smiled a hot, sensual smile that shot right to his core. "How's that?" she asked, her voice deceptively sweet.

Tru flipped the camera over in his hand and examined it with a frown. He hadn't expected such a belligerent action from her—or such an unsettling reaction from himself. And he hadn't brought a second roll of film. He looked down at the exposed ribbon, then back up at Caroline. From behind that carefully controlled exterior had emerged an unpredictable—and unphotographable—opponent.

He was probably already dead in the water, but he decided he had nothing to lose by pressing on. "There is one other thing," he began. "I promised the guys I'd bring you to our Tuesday night poker game."

"Mr. Hallihan," she said through clenched teeth. "I think you'd better leave before I—"

The intercom buzzed. She snatched up the phone and listened for a long moment. "All right, put him through." Tru watched her aggravated mood suddenly change to one of false delight. She smiled and paced back and forth behind her desk, the phone clutched in a white-knuckled hand. "Hello," she cried. "You're not really calling from an airplane over Kansas, are you?... Yes, I checked with Lance about the reception but I don't think he'll be able to make it ... he'll be out of town on business ... Another time? No, Lance is really very busy...."

His gaze wandered over her slender form and he tried to detect the details of her body hidden beneath the severe cut of her suit. She was tall and willowy and he slouched lower to examine her long legs from beneath the carved wood desk. He was definitely a leg man, and Caroline Leighton had great legs. Nothing turned him on more than trim ankles and the sweet curve of a woman's calf, the silken skin behind her knee and the long, sexy line of her thigh.

"Of course, Lance is anxious to meet you and I'm sure..."

"Lance?" Tru looked up, distracted from her legs. Who the hell was Lance? A business associate? His gaze drifted to her left hand—no wedding ring, but these days a P.I. couldn't count on that as solid evidence of marital status. The way she spoke of him, with a slight catch of affection in her voice, would lead a discerning P.I. to believe that Lance was much more than just a friend. This was an interesting new wrinkle, he mused. Could Caroline Leighton have yet another man in her life?

"Lance," he muttered. "What kind of name is that?"

Caroline held her hand over the phone. "Would you leave, please? This is a private call."

"What about my poker game?" he demanded. "I'd really enjoy a nice slice of rye toast for breakfast, and if you don't show up at my poker game, I won't be able to use my toaster."

She stared at him in bewilderment, shook her head, and returned to her phone conversation. "Lance is on the other line. If you'll hold for a few seconds, I'll check his schedule." She punched the hold button.

Placing her hands on her hips, she looked squarely at him. "You want me to put in an appearance at your poker game?"

Tru nodded, surprised.

Her eyes were sharp and discerning. "All right, I'll come to your poker game under one condition."

Tru grinned. "You name it," he said.

"You have to attend a business reception with me on Saturday night."

He shrugged. "Instead of Lance? Sure, I can do that. No problem."

She turned her attention back to the phone. "Hi, I'm back. Surprise! Saturday night is fine. Lance and I will be there. We're looking forward to meeting everyone. All right, I'll talk to you soon. Goodbye." She slowly lowered the phone and watched him pensively from behind her desk.

Tru returned her gaze. "I'm a little confused here. Why do you want me to go to a business reception with you if Lance is going?"

She sat down in her chair and leaned forward, resting her elbows on her desk and steepling her fingers in front of her. "Mr. Hallihan, you're going to be Lance for the evening."

"I'm going to stand in for your boyfriend?" Tru laughed. This was priceless and a little too hard to believe. The possible mistress of Ellis Stone was inviting him out on a date. Though his fantasy woman hadn't panned out, she had agreed to the bet. His Caddy was on its way home. He'd get his electricity back, too. And to top it all off, he'd get closer to the woman who might provide a twenty-thousand-dollar payoff.

Tru grinned. "It's a tough job, but somebody's got to do it, right?"

"Mr. Hallihan, Lance is not my boyfriend. He's my husband."

# 2

CAROLINE WATCHED Tru Hallihan squirm in his chair. She knew his type: incredibly intriguing, devastatingly handsome, and terrified by commitment. The kind of guy who refused to grow up. Just the mere mention of the word "responsibility" could set his nerves on edge and "husband" practically caused an acute panic attack. She saw it in the quick darting of his eyes—his instincts were screaming "Run, now." She wondered whether she had made the right choice. Could a man like Tru Hallihan actually be convincing as her perfectly sensitive and attentive husband, Lance? Right now, she couldn't afford to be picky.

"You're married?" He pushed himself up from his easygoing slouch and braced his elbows on his knees.

She nodded curtly while her mind hurriedly searched for a way to explain the truth.

"And you want me to pretend to be your husband?"

"That's the deal," she said, studying his features. He was a singularly sexy man and she found herself snared by his magnetic charm. His rumpled midnight black hair, and day-old beard made him look a little dangerous, so different from the well-groomed professionals she was usually attracted to. His wrinkled linen jacket hid broad shoulders and a narrow waist, and his faded jeans encased long, muscular legs. He radiated an air of absolute confidence in his strength, his good looks, and his intelligence, yet he still managed to maintain a boyish appeal.

"What will your real husband think about this?" For an instant, his hazel eyes clouded with mistrust. Obviously, he didn't usually involve himself with married women. Caroline found herself strangely pleased. Maybe Tru Hallihan also possessed at latent streak of integrity.

"Don't worry about Lance. He has no feelings one way or the other. In fact, she asked, he doesn't really exist."

Tru laughed and shook his head. He had a nice smile, Caroline thought to herself. One that lit up his eyes with a devilish sparkle. A smile he had probably used on more women than she'd care to count.

"Nice talk!" he scolded. "And you women wonder why men are so reluctant to get married. It sounds like you've got more feelings for that philodendron over there than you do for your own husband."

Caroline drew a deep breath and plunged ahead. "I have no husband, Mr. Hallihan. I used to, but we divorced three years ago. Lance is simply a product of my imagination, an example I use in my radio show, an amalgam of all the qualities women find desirable in a man."

"Let me get this straight. Lance doesn't exist. But you want me to pretend to be Lance?"

"We're both professionals here. Think of it as just another job. I've got a lot riding on this business reception and I need Lance to make an appearance. Once the reception is over, Lance can disappear back into the woodwork, where he belongs."

"Why would you want to pretend you're married? Why would *anyone* want to pretend they're married when they're not?" He stared at her, his gaze piercing through her. Realization slowly dawned across his handsome face. "Never mind. I get it now. You're a marriage counselor and you screwed up your own marriage."

"I didn't screw it up," Caroline replied. "Things just didn't work out."

"So where is Lance now? Living with his secretary in Miami Beach?"

"Edward is living in San Francisco. He's a plastic surgeon."

"Ahh. A body and fender man." Tru nodded his approval. "So who got the yacht and the house in Malibu?"

"You have a very poor opinion of marriage, Mr. Hallihan. Maybe this isn't such a good idea after all."

"I do a lot of divorce work, Dr. Leighton, and I see what marriage can do to people. One minute, you're pledging your undying love for each other, and the next, you're fighting over the crystal goblets and the designer towels . . . or having an extramarital affair," he added, raising a dark brow and studying her shrewdly.

"Not all marriages are like that. Some people believe in the institution."

"Well, I don't," he stated coldly.

"So, you don't think you'll be able to portray Lance effectively?"

"I didn't say that. I've pretended to be someone I'm not many times before. It goes along with being a P.I. Playing a devoted husband will be a new challenge, but I think I can handle it."

"Good. We have a deal then. Your poker game for my business reception. I think we'll need to meet to discuss your role in greater depth." She perused her desk calendar. "I could fit tomorrow morning into my schedule. Do you have an office?"

Tru glanced around the room as if he were cataloging the contents of hers. "No," he answered. "Not exactly."

"All right, we can meet at your apartment."

He shifted uncomfortably in his chair. "You want to meet at my apartment? Why don't we meet here?"

Typical, Caroline thought. Men always found it easier to deal with a woman on her own turf. That way if things got intolerable, they could always make a run for the door. Well, she wasn't going to let Tru Hallihan control even one factor in this deal. "No. I think it would be best if we met at your apartment," she said firmly. "The press has developed a strange obsession with Dr. Lovelace and I don't want to take unnecessary risks. If you found out I was Dr. Lovelace, anyone could."

Tru scowled. "First, Josh, and now, you! Why does everyone suddenly doubt my skills as an investigator?"

"I don't doubt your skills, I just prefer to be circumspect."

"I don't think my apartment would be—"

"Just give me your address, Mr. Hallihan." She pushed a pen and a piece of paper at him. "I understand why you find it necessary to keep your address a secret. But I'm not one of your one-night stands. This is business, and after our deal is finished, you won't need to worry about finding me on your doorstep."

"It's not that, it's just . . ."

She leveled a withering look at him. He raised his brow, then grabbed the paper and pen and scribbled down his address. Caroline took the slip of paper from his hands and retrieved her purse from her desk. She pulled out her wallet and handed him two one-hundred-dollar bills.

"What's this?"

"You'll need to rent a tux for the reception. There's a men's shop just off Rodeo Drive that rents designer tuxedos. It's called Aldus. That should be plenty to cover it. I expect you to return the change. And make sure they fit you properly. The jacket sleeves are always problematic, and the shoulders should—"

"I know how a tuxedo should fit," Tru answered. "And I know the store you're talking about."

Caroline flushed slightly. Her compulsion with control sometimes got out of control. It was what had driven Edward from their marriage, her need to analyze his every behavior, to discuss even the most minute problems, and then to offer her professional opinion. It hadn't stopped with relationship issues. She'd offered her input on every facet of Edward's life, right down to the sleeve length of his business suits and the men's stores at which he shopped.

She had been taught from an early age to take control of her own life, to examine every problem she encountered and devise a logical way to solve it. Her parents admired independence and encouraged her to articulate her beliefs and opinions. And from the time she'd spoken her first words, they had listened to her as if she were an adult. She'd grown up with a strong sense of self-determination and a stubborn insistence on perfection.

She had tried so hard to make her marriage work, always keeping the lines of communication open, but somewhere along the road to perfection, she had sent her husband running in the opposite direction. When the fire had died between them, Edward had preferred to keep warm with another woman.

"All right. I'll see you tomorrow morning, then." She held out her hand.

Tru glanced down, then looked back into her eyes, a rakish grin curling his firm mouth. "I like this idea," he teased, as he clasped her hand in his. "All the benefits of marriage without the commitment. It's a concept that might just catch on."

A shiver shot up her spine at his suggestive innuendo and an image of Tru Hallihan, lying naked in her bed, flashed in her mind. Lord, she had been too long without a man. Even a scoundrel like Tru Hallihan was starting to look good. "There won't be any *benefits*," she snapped, "beyond my appearance at your poker game. Let's make that point very clear from the start. And there won't be any return engagements."

He squeezed her hand. "You never know."

She pulled her hand from his and rubbed her palms together. "My nine o'clock will be here any minute. I'd appreciate it if you would keep this arrangement confidential."

"Confidential's my middle name. I'll think of you as one of my clients," Tru replied as he walked toward the door. He stopped and turned around, bracing his shoulder against the doorjamb. "There's just one more thing."

"What is that, Mr. Hallihan?"

"If Lance doesn't really exist, can't we at least change his name? I have a hard time relating to that name. How about Rick? Or Joe? Those are real 'guy' names. Lance sounds like your hairdresser's name."

Caroline had to admit it was hard to imagine the simmering masculinity of Tru Hallihan in the body of a man named Lance. "We'll discuss that tomorrow morning."

He grinned. "Maybe you ought to consider 'Tru.'"

With that, he turned and she watched him stride through her reception area and out the front door. Caroline stood in the door of her office for a long time, considering the events of the past thirty minutes. She'd never met a man quite like Tru Hallihan. Buried somewhere beneath the roguish bravado, she sensed an honest and sincere individual, a person he tried hard to hide.

"Tru," she murmured to herself, liking the sound of his name. As she turned back into her office, well satisfied with herself, she made a mental note to scratch "husband" from her "to do" list.

TRU SLIPPED HIS KEY into the security lock of the front door at the Bachelor Arms and, balancing a six-pack of beer and a bag of take-out Chinese against his chest, pulled the door open. Life was good. He didn't even care if he opened his apartment door to find another bill on the floor. His fortunes had taken a turn for the better since he had met Dr. Caroline Leighton.

Using Caroline's tux rental money, he had ransomed his car from the service shop an hour after he left her office. After that, the day seemed to fall into place. With renewed enthusiasm, he tracked down a few deadbeat clients and by noon, he had collected enough to pay his electric bill. A personal visit to the power company office and an impassioned plea involving a sick grandmother got his power promptly turned back on.

On his way home, he stopped by Aldus, the trendy men's store that he knew quite well. Theodore Smith, the dapper, middle-aged tenant in 2-F, worked as a sales associate there and often gave the male tenants at the Arms insider information on upcoming designer markdowns. Though Garrett McCabe bought most of his clothes at Aldus, Tru preferred The Gap. Josh Banks shopped exclusively at the very conservative Brooks Brothers.

After choosing a sleek Armani tux, Tru talked Theodore into using his in-store influence to "borrow" the tux for the weekend, in return for the use of Tru's classic '57 Cadillac convertible the following weekend. Theodore was quite the ladies' man, but his economy car did little to enhance his man-about-town image.

In less than a day, all Tru's financial problems were solved with only a couple hundred dollars cash and some shrewd bartering. The payout on his two poker bets would be pure profit. Tru walked across the tiny lobby and down the hall toward his apartment.

The Arms was originally a luxurious mansion, built by a wealthy family in the early days of Hollywood. When the family fell on hard times in the late twenties, the building was divided into three spacious and posh apartments, homes to some of Hollywood's hottest male movie stars—all of them bachelors. The complex was soon dubbed the Bachelor Arms and became well-known for its wild parties.

Eventually, the apartments were subdivided into smaller units, and the pool in the Spanish-style courtyard was filled with dirt and concrete. Still, the sun-bleached pink stucco and turquoise trim, red tile roofs and wrought iron balconies, the lush, tropical courtyard garden, all combined to give the apartments the feel of an oasis in the middle of busy L.A. Though Tru rented just a tiny studio apartment, he wouldn't consider living anywhere else. The place seemed to resonate with all the lost glamour and intrigue of Hollywood. What better place for a P.I. who cut his teeth on Raymond Chandler and his detective novel hero, Philip Marlow.

As Tru passed 1-G, he noticed that the door was open. He stopped and looked inside the apartment, a spacious, and vacant, one-bedroom. Since when had 1-G been empty? He had asked the manager, Ken Amberson, to let him know when a larger apartment became available, but Ken hadn't said a word about 1-G.

Tru set his beer and food down outside the door and walked in. He turned slowly as he took in each detail of the apartment. This was exactly what he was looking for and with his financial situation looking up, he'd be able to afford the increase in rent. He stopped as his gaze reached the far wall of the living room. Next to a small arched window hung an immense mirror, nearly five feet tall and almost as wide. Slowly, he walked across the room and examined the ornate pewter frame.

He reached out and ran his finger along the finely formed metal. Grabbing the bottom corners of the mirror, he tried to pull it away from the wall, but it wouldn't budge. Tru stared long and hard at his reflection. He'd never seen the mirror before, but somehow he knew that this was the one they whispered about.

He shook his head and brushed off the strange sense of foreboding that seemed to hang in the air. The story had been told several times in his presence, but he had never paid attention to the details. So many outlandish legends swirled around the history of the Bachelor Arms, everything from drunken brawls to orgies to suicide to murder. But the mirror had a story all its own. He just couldn't recall what it was.

"Thinking about indulging in a shave and a decent haircut?"

Drawn out of his speculation, Tru looked up to see Theodore Smith's perfectly groomed reflection beside his in the mirror.

"I didn't know this unit was empty again," Theodore said as he examined himself critically in the silvered glass. He smoothed the graying hair at his temples and ran his fingers over an imaginary wrinkle in his forehead. Theodore always appreciated a mirror and flattering lighting. It gave him yet another opportunity to preen.

"I didn't either," Tru said. "So, what do you think?"

"Plastic surgery," he replied softly. "I'm thinking of having my eyes done." He pulled the skin under his eyes tight. "What do you think? Does it make me look younger?"

"I meant, what do you think about the mirror?"

Theodore frowned and shrugged. "It doesn't make me look any better than any other mirror, so I'm not particularly fond of it. Why would someone leave this behind? It looks like an antique."

"I'm not sure anyone has," Tru replied. "Have you heard any of the old stories about this place? Any stories about a mirror like this?"

"No, should I have?"

Tru chuckled and relaxed. "I guess not." He turned and looked at the garment bag that Theodore had thrown over his shoulder. "Is that my tux?"

Theodore handed him the bag. "Armani. Three thousand dollars retail. Don't go spilling any marinara sauce on it or my boss will have my head. I included a pleated shirt and a bow tie. One of those pre-tied numbers. I figured you wouldn't know how to tie a real one. I assume you don't own a set of studs and cuff links?"

"If they don't go on a T-shirt, I don't own 'em," Tru said.

"You can borrow mine," Theodore said. "Stop by tomorrow morning and I'll give them to you." He looked at his watch. "I've got to go. I have a dinner date tonight with Jill Foyle, the Linda Evans look-alike from 2-B. Wish me luck." As he walked toward the door, Tru's attention returned to the mirror.

"Hey," Tru called, distractedly watching Theodore's retreating reflection in the mirror. "Thanks. I really appreciate this."

Theodore looked over his shoulder and smiled. "She must be pretty special to get you into a tux."

He laughed. "Yeah, she's special," he said dryly. "Special doesn't even come close to covering it."

She was special, all right, with her uptight, button-down facade and that sexy voice, that thick chestnut hair pulled back in a tidy little knot, and those long legs. But there was something more about her, something he couldn't put his finger on. What a strange twist of fate that she might be the target of his investigation, the mysterious mistress of Ellis Stone. It was probably just his investigative instincts that drew him to her, and nothing more.

As Theodore's footsteps faded in the hallway, Tru stared hard at his reflection. A strange image shifted and wavered before his eyes and he realized it wasn't just a mental image of Dr. Caroline Leighton.

Tru blinked hard. The face of a stranger stared out at him from the reflective depths of the mirror—a black-haired woman who bore no resemblance to any woman he had ever met before. She stared at him for a long moment, studying him as intently as he did her. Then, as if she approved of what she saw, she smiled. He turned his head and looked behind him, but the room was empty.

When he turned back to the mirror, the image was gone.

"Got your electricity back, huh."

Startled, Tru spun around and came face-to-face with the building superintendent, Ken Amberson. The man stood in the middle of the room in a spot that had been empty just a moment before.

"Hello, Ken," he murmured, wondering if he had somehow mistaken Ken's reflection for a woman's. Tru had dealt with a lot of weird types in his career as a P.I., but no one as strange as Amberson. He seemed to appear out of nowhere, then disappeared just as suddenly. And he had an uncanny knack for knowing every detail of every tenant's life. Tru suspected he went through the garbage or had bugged all the apartments, but he had never been able to prove his suspicions.

"Power company been here an hour ago," Ken stated in his emotionless voice.

"Good. Thanks. There was a screwup with my bill and they shut the power off by mistake."

Ken stared at him through shrewd eyes, as if waiting for either further explanation or a change of subject. Tru decided to oblige the latter. "I noticed this apartment was vacant. I thought you were going to let me know when a larger unit became available."

"Who said this place was vacant?" he said, instantly suspicious.

Tru glanced around. "I don't see anyone living here. Are you planning to rent this out or not?"

Ken glanced over at the mirror nervously. "Haven't decided."

Amberson fancied himself as important as a battlefield general, in command of all those who billeted at the Bachelor Arms. He ran the complex like his own little empire, a modern day Napoleon, right down to his diminutive height and his autocratic attitude.

"Well, let me know, would you?" Tru said, irritated. "I'd be interested in getting a bigger place."

Ken nodded, as if dismissing an incompetent subordinate. Taking his cue, Tru crossed the room and walked through the door. He turned back to restate his interest, but the door silently swung closed, as if the Little General had willed it from across the room.

Tru glanced around uneasily. Geez, the guy gave him the creeps.

CAROLINE STOOD at the door of apartment 2-E, tapping her foot impatiently. She glanced at her watch, then knocked again, this time with more authority. No answer. Where could he be? They had an appointment. She pulled a neatly folded piece of paper from her purse and double-checked the address. Yes, she was at the right apartment and yes, this was Saturday morning. She'd rung the security buzzer three times before she decided to sneak in with another tenant and try Tru's apartment door.

She pounded harder, more in frustration than in hope of getting an answer. Of all the irresponsible, immature—

"What the hell is so damn important?" The door swung open beneath her fist and Tru Hallihan appeared in the doorway, rumpled from sleep and visibly irritated. Still badly in need of a shave, he looked as disreputable as ever in a worn T-shirt and a pair of wildly patterned baggy shorts that nearly reached his knees. He squinted at her then scrubbed at his eyes. After a long moment, he seemed to recognize her and his expression calmed a bit.

"I woke you up," she stated. As if that weren't obvious, she thought. But she was unable to think of anything else to say, faced with his disheveled and innately sexy appearance.

"What was your first clue?" Tru grumbled, stepping aside so she could enter.

"We *did* have an appointment," she said stubbornly. "Did you forget?"

He left her standing near the front door and wandered in the direction of a small kitchen, yawning and stretching along the way. "I've got to make coffee. I must have overslept. What time is it?" She heard him turn on the faucet.

"Seven o'clock."

He poked his head out the kitchen doorway and stared at her as if she'd just told him the moon was made of Swiss cheese. "Seven o'clock? Tell me you don't mean a.m."

So she had been a bit overly anxious to get started. After all, she only had a short time to turn Tru Hallihan into husband material. And from what she could see of his apartment, she could use far more than just a morning. It looked like his closet had exploded. Clothes were draped over every piece of furniture, and shoes and socks were scattered across the floor. She didn't even want to see the kitchen, much less the bathroom.

He stood in the doorway raking his fingers through his spiky hair. "I take that back. I didn't oversleep. When you said Saturday morning, I assumed you meant nine or ten o'clock. Who in their right mind gets up this early on a Saturday morning?"

"I do," Caroline replied defensively. "Lying in bed all day is a waste of valuable time. Morning is a very productive time for me. I get up and I make a list of all the things I have to do." She glanced around the apartment. "Shopping, errands . . . housework."

"I gave the maid the year off," Tru said. "Sue me."

"I just meant that on Saturday mornings I'm refreshed and my energy is high," she added, trying to cover her indirect insult.

"I guess the lack of a social life can do that to you," he said in mock sympathy. He walked across the room and handed her the coffeepot. "If you've got so much energy, you can make the coffee. I like it strong. I'm going to take a shower. I'll be out in a few minutes."

Still piqued by his astute comment about her nonexistent social life, Caroline watched him head for the bathroom. She placed her briefcase on the cluttered dining room table, then slowly turned to examine Tru Hallihan's habitat.

The sleeper couch was a tangle of sheets, pillows and blankets, and the lone chair in the room was an enormous recliner, a standard fixture in any bachelor pad. The seat was stacked with newspapers. Tru obviously considered reading material and electronic equipment more important than furniture. One entire wall was filled with stereo equipment and a huge television. Another wall was lined with shelves, crammed from floor to ceiling with books. She carefully picked her way between shoes and stacks of magazines to skim the shelves. Thoreau, Melville, Hawthorne, and complete collections of Shakespeare and Dickens. And above that, a shelf stuffed with old detective novels. Not the kind of reading Caroline would have expected from Tru Hallihan. He seemed more like the girlie-magazine type.

She was tempted to tidy up, not for his sake, but because she hated to work in such chaos. But, sensing Tru's aversion to any female interference in his life, she didn't want to appear too presumptuous—or pushy. Besides, she wasn't the one who needed practice playing the caring and sensitive mate.

With a final futile look around the room, she decided to venture into the kitchen and make coffee. Surprisingly, this room was spotless. She learned why when she opened the refrigerator. It was empty, except for a bag of gourmet coffee beans, a jar of grape jelly, four cans of beer, and a jug of milk with a expiration date a month past. The freezer held a loaf of bread and a selection of ice cream that would rival most ice-cream parlors. The man had at least one weakness.

After preparing the coffee and pouring a mug for herself, she cleared a spot at the tiny dining table, sat down and waited. Within minutes, Tru appeared, freshly showered but still unshaven, his hair slicked back and curling damply against his neck. If it weren't for the dark shadow of his beard, and the T-shirt and torn jeans, he might almost look respectable. He grinned seductively and she changed her mind. Almost respectable, but not quite trustworthy.

"You didn't happen to bring along any donuts, did you?"

She shook her head.

"I guess they weren't on your list." He went to pour himself a mug of coffee, then pulled out a chair, turned it around and straddled it. "So, what's up . . ." He raised his brows and sipped his coffee. ". . . Doc?"

She folded her hands in front of her and collected her thoughts. "We have to put together a strategy for tonight. I want you to be prepared. Since this is the first time I'm going to meet most of these people, they'll be most interested in talking to me. Your presence there is just a formality, so you won't have to say much. Just stay by my side and agree with everything I say."

"Sort of like a trained chimp?"

Caroline felt her face flush. That's exactly what she meant, but she couldn't say that. Not to Tru Hallihan. "No! Not at all. Just try to blend in and let me take the lead. It will be safer that way."

"And you like to play it safe, don't you?" He watched her over the rim of his coffee mug, his perceptive gaze a strange but mesmerizing mixture of green and brown.

"I don't make ridiculous poker bets, if that's what you mean."

Sparks of humor glittered in his eyes. "Ridiculous? It can't be that ridiculous. You agreed to fulfill the bet, didn't you? And I'll wager you make it a point never to act ridiculous."

"Mr. Hallihan—"

"Tru," he said in a deceptively smooth voice. "After all, we are husband and wife."

"Then I should call you Lance."

Tru made a distasteful face. "I hate that name. Makes me sound like a sissy pants."

Caroline smiled and tried to suppress a laugh. "And I'll wager you make it a point never to sound like a sissy pants, right?"

He tipped his coffee mug to her and chuckled, the sound like a warm embrace inviting her to relax for a brief, but delicious moment. "Touché, darling. That's why I married you. For your brilliant wit and sparkling sense of humor."

"I think we'd better get to work on Lance. Why don't we start with the basics?" She opened her briefcase and withdrew a pen and a legal pad, then pushed both across the table to him. He looked at her questioningly. "I've made a—a list of a few facts that you may need to know. You might want to take notes as we talk."

He flipped through the legal pad. "A *few* facts? You've practically written a book on the guy. For a man who doesn't exist, Lance has taken on a life of his own." He shoved the pad aside.

"Aren't you going to study those notes?"

"I have a photographic memory," Tru replied. "What does Lance do?"

Caroline frowned. "Nothing. I mean, I don't think I've ever mentioned his career on the radio. We'll have to make up a career for him."

"Good. How about private investigator?" he volunteered.

Caroline shook her head. "No, that won't work."

"Why not?"

She hesitated. Why did he have to challenge everything she said? Why couldn't he be a cooperative and complacent husband? "I just wouldn't...I mean, it wouldn't be logical..." She knew she'd have to complete her thought. Tru Hallihan wouldn't let her get by with such a haphazard evasion. She took a deep breath. "A private investigator just wouldn't be my...type. Do you have any other area of expertise?" she asked, hoping to deflect a snide comeback.

"I'm an expert at a lot of things," he teased. "But most of them have less to do with work and more to do with play."

Her face warmed again. All right, maybe he was an expert in basketball or golf, she thought. Why did she always read something sexual into his comments? Because, that's exactly how he intended them to be taken, she asserted. Tru was determined to shake her resolve and she was letting him get away with it.

"Mr. Hallihan," she began, her voice cool. He arched a dark brow. "Tru," she amended, "I'd prefer to keep this on a purely business level. I'm not interested in your prowess with the ladies."

"My *prowess?*"

She nodded.

He grinned. "I like that word. Prowess. Let me write that word down." He scribbled it on the legal pad then stared at it. "I was referring to my softball skills. I'm a terrific hitter. I always get to first base."

She fixed him with a exasperated frown. She would not let him bait her like this.

"I have a Ph.D. in English literature from Stanford," he said in a pretentious but playful tone. "It didn't prepare me for much beyond academia, but it might be useful to Lance."

"You have a Ph.D.?" Caroline asked in disbelief.

"Don't sound so shocked. We're all allowed to make a few impractical choices in our life."

"I—I'm not shocked. Well, maybe I am, a little. Why didn't you teach?"

"A doctoral dissertation on American detective novels. And a fondness for Raymond Chandler, Dashiell Hammett and Mickey Spillane. Besides, I'm not the kind of guy who would fit in with all that ivy and tweed."

"No, I guess you wouldn't." Caroline tapped her finger distractedly against her coffee mug. "You could always be a nuclear physicist. It's impressive, but it borders on being politically incorrect. No one will ask questions. And if they do, just tell them you work for the government on some top secret project that you can't talk about. These guys will either be incredibly bored and ignore you, or be terribly intimidated and hope you won't make them look stupid."

"I'm amazed," Tru exclaimed. "You've got quite a flair for both logic and lying, Dr. Leighton."

"It's not lying," Caroline replied. "Not exactly."

Tru pushed out of his chair and headed toward the kitchen. "What do you call it then?"

She searched for the words. "Protecting my options," she finally said.

"Who exactly are these guys you're trying to fool?"

She hesitated for a moment, wondering how much she needed to tell him. He had promised to keep all she told him confidential, but she wasn't sure how far she could trust him. "They're executives for a television distribution syndicate. I've been approached about turning my radio show into a television talk show. Though many marriage counselors are divorced, the producer and the syndicate executives might be overly concerned over that particular point. I don't want anything so minor to get in the way of this opportunity."

"How long do you think you can keep this up?" he called from the kitchen.

"Just long enough to show them what I can do. After that, I can tell them the truth. It won't make any difference by then. And if it doesn't work out, I haven't done anything to compromise my practice. That is, as long as you don't tell anyone about this."

He stood in the kitchen doorway and leaned against the doorjamb. "A writer," Tru said.

She turned to him. "What?"

"Lance can be a writer," he said. "An aspiring author who toils at writing the great American detective novel. Or how about a struggling screenwriter? There are plenty of those in this town."

Caroline considered his suggestion. It wasn't a bad idea and it cleared up any technical hang-ups. Certainly, a Ph.D. in English literature could pretend to be a struggling writer. "All right, screenwriter will work. If they think you've got a script to sell, they'll probably avoid you like the plague." She sighed inwardly. One task down and hundreds more to go. Trying to turn Tru into

Lance was an exhausting process, a battle of wits and clever comebacks that she wasn't sure she'd survive. They'd never cover everything in one morning.

"I'm not so sure about this," she said, turning away from him. "I made a list of pros and cons for this plan and on paper it looked good, but now I'm not so sure. Maybe I should just tell Ellis the truth and take my chances. There are just too many ways for this to fail."

"Ellis?" Tru asked, his voice sharp.

She turned to catch an uneasy expression cross his face. "Yes, Ellis Stone. Do you know him?"

Tru shrugged. "No . . . I mean, I've heard of him. Who hasn't? He's a big mover and shaker in town."

"Ellis is the head of the production company that's interested in producing my show. He's a very understanding man. I'm sure if I told him I was divorced he would—"

"Come on, Caroline," Tru chided. "You can't back out now. You can't take that chance."

The sound of her name soft on his lips startled her and she closed her eyes, attempting to gather her resolve. If it were any other man, she was certain she could succeed. But Tru Hallihan was a disaster waiting to happen and she knew she shouldn't trust him with something as important as her future. She was even beginning to wonder if she could trust herself in his presence. He had a peculiar talent for unnerving her.

He came up behind her and placed his hands on her shoulders, his touch light and undemanding. "Tell me about your perfect husband, Caroline."

She tried to ignore the gentle heat of his fingers but the warmth spread through her body like a fine cognac, liquid and tranquilizing. She stood up and slipped from the realm of his tantalizing touch. "All right," she said, trying to control her shaky voice by pacing back and forth. "Lance is—I mean, he would be—sensitive and caring. A man who would put my needs and my feelings before his own."

"Ah, a spineless wimp," Tru said, straddling his chair again.

"No, not a wimp," she replied calmly. "There's nothing wrong with a man who shows his sensitive side."

"Nothing except the big heel mark on his chest from constantly getting stepped on by women."

She looked at his chest, broad and muscular, outlined by the tight T-shirt. She couldn't imagine stepping on that chest. But she could imagine touching and— With a silent curse, she reined in her imagination and her hormones. "Are you speaking from experience or ignorance?"

He shrugged. "Just plain old common sense. The way I look at it, a real man is sort of like Mexican food."

"Mexican food?" Though carrying on a conversation with Tru was sometimes baffling, it was always entertaining. "All right, I'll bite," she said. "How are real men like Mexican food?"

"You know how Mexican food is spicy and hot and it tastes real good? Even though you know you're going to pay the price later, it doesn't stop you from wanting just one more burrito. Now sensitive guys, they're like oatmeal, good for you, but kind of bland and boring. Tell me, Dr. Leighton, which would you rather have?"

Oatmeal, Caroline said to herself. At least that's what she'd always found herself drawn to. But Tru was right— a steady diet of the stuff didn't make for a very exciting love life. Edward had been oatmeal when they had married, and she had tried to turn him into something even more bland. Maybe she should consider giving Mexican food a chance. Just a taste, to see if she liked it.

"I think we're getting off the subject," she said. "I've portrayed Lance as a man who's very open with his emotions and his concerns. If you're going to be Lance, you're going to have to act more sensitive and caring."

"You want me to cry?" Tru asked.

"No," she said emphatically.

"Then maybe I should just get a little misty when I tell that story of how we met? How did we meet, by the way?"

"I want you to take this seriously. I've got a lot riding on this reception and if you're going to treat this like some big joke, I'd have better luck with some narrow-minded Neanderthal."

He smiled sardonically. "But isn't that what I am?"

Caroline clenched her fists and closed her eyes, drawing a deep, steadying breath. "No," she said as she opened her eyes. "I think you want everyone to believe you are, but you're not. I think, deep down inside, you're a sensitive, caring man."

He clutched his chest. "Ouch! You wound me, Caroline."

She glared at him until his expression became adequately contrite. "Are you ready to get down to work, or should we just forget this whole thing?" she demanded.

"I'm ready," he said, spreading his arms wide and tipping his head back in supplication. "Go ahead, Dr. Leighton, I'm putty in your hands. Transform me into your one and only."

She shook her head. She had to be crazy to think she could pull this off. Tru Hallihan was not a man who could be considered malleable by any stretch of the imagination. Caroline inhaled sharply. Still, that didn't make him less attractive.

In fact, as crazy as it sounded, she kind of liked him just the way he was.

# 3

FLYNN'S WAS RELATIVELY quiet for an early Saturday evening. Tru had promised Theodore that he would stop by his apartment for a final check by the chief of the fashion police before he left to pick up Caroline. When there was no answer at 2-F, he figured Theodore would be found sipping chardonnay on his favorite bar stool. As Tru stood in the doorway of Flynn's, he saw Theodore—flanked by Garrett and Josh. Bob Robinson sat on his usual corner stool and Eddie was behind the bar. Tru had already decided to leave, not wanting to explain his formal attire to his friends, when he caught Garrett's eye.

His friend's voice boomed across the bar. "Hold the elevator," he shouted. "What have we here?"

Every eye turned toward him. Tru shot Garrett an annoyed glare before he walked over to where they sat and slid onto the stool next to Garrett. Playing it cool, he ordered a beer and waited for the interrogation to begin.

"So who died?" Garrett quipped.

"One doesn't wear an Armani tux to a funeral," Theodore scolded. "Truman's got a date. He says she's special. Isn't that what you said, Tru?"

"Special?" Garrett asked. "She'd have to be drop-dead gorgeous for our Truman to get himself all decked out like this. Is she an actress or a model? He must be going to one of those award ceremonies. So, who is she Tru? And can I have her phone number after she dumps you?"

Tru took a long swallow of his beer. "You wouldn't believe me if I told you."

"Try me," Garrett replied.

Tru was tempted to spill his guts and give them the whole lowdown on the mysterious Carly Lovelace. But for some unfathomable reason, he wanted to keep her to himself just a little bit longer. He had spent the entire morning exploring Lance's psyche and circuitously learning what Caroline Leighton looked for in a man. By the end of their meeting, he felt as if he knew more about her than he had known about any other woman he had ever met.

He found it increasingly hard to believe that she was having an affair with a married man, especially a man like Ellis Stone. If she was, why would she be trying so hard to keep the truth of her marital status from a man she was sleeping with? It didn't make sense. If there *was* anything going on between them, he knew he'd be able to spot it tonight. And if there wasn't, then he was back to square one. As ridiculous as it sounded, he couldn't help but hope that would be the case—that she wasn't Ellis Stone's mistress.

He sort of liked her. She was different from the women he usually dated. Not that he was actually dating her, because he wasn't. And not because she wasn't attractive, because she was. Any fool could see through that businesslike veneer. Those green eyes and those delicate upswept lashes. That thick, shiny hair, brushing a long, graceful neck. And that voice—God, that voice—that could make any man shiver with lust.

But there was more. He wanted to believe that she was incapable of the deceit necessary to carry on an affair with Stone. He wanted to know that she was a woman worth trusting. No, Caroline was not going to become the subject of idle barroom conversation. At least, not tonight.

"Later," Tru replied. "So, Theodore, what do you think? Can I swing with the big boys in this getup?" He pushed away from the bar and stood up to strike a *GQ* pose, then slowly turned around.

Theodore eyed him critically. "The pants fit like they were made for you, but the jacket binds a bit across the shoulders. As long as you're not planning to lift weights in that tux, you'll be all right. You aren't planning to bench press a few hundred pounds tonight, are you?"

"Don't worry," Tru said. "Where I'm going, the heaviest thing I'll be lifting will be a champagne glass."

"Come on, Tru," Bob said. "Tell us all about this mystery lady."

Tru shook his head and took another swig of his beer. He'd keep this mystery lady to himself for just a little while longer. But there was another woman he did want to learn more about.

"Not that I'm anxious to change the subject," Tru said, "but have you guys seen anyone moving in or out of 1-G?"

"Is that the place with the mirror?" Theodore asked.

"What mirror?" Bob asked.

"I haven't seen anyone going in or out of that place for months," Garrett said. "Why?"

"I told Ken Amberson that I wanted a bigger place and he assured me that as soon as a one-bedroom unit opened up, he'd let me know. Yesterday afternoon I walked past 1-G and it was empty, except for this huge mirror on the wall."

"How huge?" Bob asked.

Tru shrugged. "I don't know, maybe four by five feet. It's got a real fancy frame, too. Isn't there some kind of old story floating around about a mirror? I remember hearing something but I can't recall what it was. And Amberson seemed real jumpy, like he was trying to hide something."

"That must be it," Bob murmured.

"What?" Tru asked.

"Well," Bob began, "I'm not saying that I believe all the crazy stories, but not long ago there was a rumor flying around that the place was haunted. Since I've been coming to this bar, I've met three guys who have lived in 1-G and they've all mysteriously moved out after two or three months. Seems some of the tenants have seen a strange reflection in the mirror."

The hair on the back of Tru's neck suddenly stood on end.

"Tru sees a strange reflection in the mirror every morning," Garrett joked. "It's just his ugly mug."

"What kind of reflection?" Tru asked.

"It's the reflection of some woman," Bob explained. "Maybe she's a ghost. She's dressed in a long gown and she looks at you like she can see right into your soul. The story goes that when someone sees that reflection, their greatest fear is about to be realized."

Tru frowned.

"That's strange," Eddie said. "I heard that when someone sees the woman, their greatest dream will come true."

Bob frowned. "No, I'm sure it's their greatest fear."

"And I'm sure it's their greatest dream," Eddie countered.

"So which is it?" Tru asked.

Bob shrugged and ordered another beer. "I guess it doesn't really matter. Unless you see the reflection, of course."

"You didn't see the reflection, did you?" Josh asked.

Tru shook his head. "No, no. I was just curious. I remembered hearing the stories, but I couldn't remember the specifics."

"Well, I think it's all a bunch of bull," Bob said. "Amberson probably made the whole story up. He's a weird egg, that guy is. Always mumbling to himself. Gives me the creeps."

"Me, too," Eddie said. "He's got those eerie eyes. Gives me the willies. He doesn't come in here often, but when he does, I give him a wide berth."

Tru gulped down the rest of his beer, then tossed two dollars onto the bar. He suddenly felt like the walls were closing in on him. He had seen the woman in the mirror. He hadn't imagined it. "Listen, I've got to get going. I'll see you guys later."

"Hey, how are you doing with our bet?" Garrett asked. "Did you find the real Dr. Carly Lovelace?"

"Yeah," Tru said distractedly. "I found her."

"So is she coming to the poker game on Tuesday?" Josh asked.

"Yeah," Tru said as he headed toward the door. "She'll be there."

"Hey, wait a minute," Garrett called. "We want to know more. Who is she?"

"I have to go," Tru said. "I'll talk to you later."

He couldn't get outside fast enough. Once he hit the sidewalk, he drew a long breath. The story was ridiculous. He didn't believe in ghosts and he hadn't seen anything in the mirror. He had just been tired and stressed out and mistaken Amberson's reflection for something else. Maybe it was all a trick. The guy probably enjoyed deliberately spooking people with that mirror.

Still, Tru couldn't shake the feeling that something, or someone, had intruded into his life. His deepest fear or his greatest dream. So, which was it?

He sighed and started toward his car. At least he was safe for tonight, he rationalized. Though Caroline Leighton was attractive, she certainly couldn't be classified as his dream girl. And he didn't have anything to fear from her, except maybe another three or four hours of her lessons in human husbandry and her never-ending lists.

The story was ridiculous, he repeated to himself as he hopped into his Caddy. He didn't believe in ghosts.

Tru glanced over his shoulder, then pulled out into traffic. The night was warm and breezy, a perfect end to a sun-drenched September day. He took his time driving up into the hills above the city, enjoying the evening— the plaintive calls of the night birds and the rustle of the breeze in the palms. By the time he found Caroline's Laurel Canyon home, he was already a half hour late.

"You're late," Caroline said as she pulled open the front door. She had a keen talent for stating the obvious. He ignored her irritated frown and sauntered into the huge, airy foyer. The home was an incredible piece of architecture, built on a hillside and constructed of redwood and glass. Though it wasn't particularly large, the open layout of the rooms and the all-white furniture gave it a spacious feeling. Dr. Leighton lived in comfort and style.

Tru turned back to Caroline. "And you're—" His smart comeback died in his throat. "—beautiful." His gaze drifted along the length of her body. She wore a simple sleeveless black dress with a high neckline and cutaway shoulders that bared her graceful arms from the base of her neck to her fingertips. The hemline ended five inches above her knee, showing off her incredible legs. And in between her neck and knees, the soft fabric of her dress molded to the curves of her breasts and hips and backside. Her dark hair was again pulled back into a prissy knot at her nape, but it looked more sophisticated than schoolmarmish. "You look—wow—you look terrific," he said.

"Very good," she replied with a curt nod. "I see you studied the list I gave you. A woman always enjoys compliments on her appearance. Especially from her husband."

Tru smiled. "I wasn't pretending, Caroline. I was being honest. You do look terrific."

She glanced away uneasily. "And you look very nice, too," she murmured. "I see you decided to shave."

Tru rubbed his jaw. "Yeah, I thought it was about time," he said. He held out his arms. "So what do you think of the monkey suit?"

She rotated a slender manicured finger and he turned around slowly. He felt her palms smooth across his shoulders and tug at the back of his jacket. When he met her gaze again, her brow was furrowed. "The jacket's a little tight."

Tru shrugged. "So Lance isn't always the model of sartorial splendor. The guy is human, after all. Give him a break."

His words seemed to strike a sour chord in her and her temper blazed to life in her green eyes. "What's that supposed to mean?" she asked, jumping to the defense.

"Nothing," he said, backing down.

"No, tell me," she demanded. "Lance would be honest. He'd tell me exactly what he was thinking. Honest communication is the cornerstone of a good marriage."

Tru studied her for a long moment then shrugged. "It just means that I pity any guy who tries to live up to your high standards, Dr. Leighton."

Though Tru hadn't a clue as to what caused her intense reaction, he felt a small measure of satisfaction at her indignant expression. He liked seeing Caroline in a high emotional state. After all, someone had to rattle her cool and composed cage every now and then. She was much too uptight for her own good—and his.

"And if your standards got any lower," she countered smoothly. "I'd be able to stack all *three* on top of each other and slide them under my front door, with plenty of room to spare."

Tru shook his head. "Our first fight as husband and wife. This is a momentous occasion. Can we kiss and make up now?"

She glared at him. "We are not fighting. And we are not husband and wife! You're playing a role and if you can't play it effectively, then our deal is off. No Lance, no poker game."

Tru stepped in front of her and gently clasped her upper arms. Her skin was silken beneath his fingers and he rubbed his palms up and down, enjoying the warm velvety feel of her body and the sweet flowery scent that surrounded her. "I'm sorry, *darling*," he murmured in a properly apologetic voice. "I didn't mean to upset you. What I said was insensitive and ill-mannered and I hope you'll forgive me."

She looked at him suspiciously, then reluctantly took his lead. "And I'm sorry, too. I guess I'm just a little tense about tonight. I didn't mean to snap at you . . . *dear*."

Tru bent over and brushed a chaste kiss on her cheek. "I think I'm going to be sick," he muttered into her ear. "All these sugary apologies are bad for my system."

"I'm sure you'll survive," Caroline replied as she pulled away. She gathered her wrap and her purse from an upholstered settee, then turned to him and took a deep breath. "Are you ready?"

He nodded. "Yeah, let's get this show on the road."

"I mean, are you ready for tonight? Did you really study that list I gave you, or are you just faking it?"

"If you can't tell, then I guess it doesn't make any difference, does it?" he replied.

"When is my birthday?" she inquired.

"February fifth," he replied.

"Our anniversary?"

Tru raised his brow. "Though, like most husbands, the date usually eludes me, we were married nine years ago, on May seventh at a small church in your hometown of Westport, Connecticut. Your college roommate was maid of honor and my brother, Bill, was best man. We had the wedding luncheon at your parents' country club." He smiled. "Seafood Newburg in those little pastry things and cheesecake for dessert, wasn't it?"

"That's not what we had to eat," she said.

He pulled her wrap from her hands and draped it over her shoulders. "So, I made that part up," he said. "Now that I've told you about the wedding, why don't you give me all the details about the honeymoon? We did have a good time, didn't we?"

He opened the front door for her and she stepped outside. "We spent a week in Paris," she replied. "It was very nice."

He turned her toward him and gave her a shocked look. "Very *nice*? Darling, the food on the plane was *nice*. The weather was *nice*. Our honeymoon was extraordinary. Earth-shattering." He wrapped his arms around her waist and looked down into her wide eyes. "We spent the entire week in our hotel room making mad, passionate love to each other. You were insatiable. I was exhausted. We lived on love and champagne. Don't you remember?"

She pulled away and walked toward the driveway. "That's not how I remember it," she called over her shoulder.

He followed her, then grabbed her hand and tucked it in the crook of his arm. "Too bad. But it could have been that way. With the right guy."

"I was with the right guy. My husband, Edward. And we had a very...lovely time."

She glanced away and Tru stifled a smile. Caroline was a terrible liar, especially when it came to her former marriage and her ex-husband. He doubted if any man had ever experienced the true extent of Caroline's passion. It would take someone very patient and persistent to find the real woman beneath that icy shell. Edward had given up way too early. If he *had* discovered the real Caroline, he wouldn't have let her go.

"We visited the museums and strolled the Rive Gauche," she chattered on. "And we ate at some of the finest restaurants in the city. It was all very romantic. Maybe I should write this all down for you."

"No need. I can imagine the details. It was all very proper and very tame and just a little boring, right?"

She stopped suddenly and snatched her hand from his arm. "No. Edward and I enjoyed ourselves thoroughly."

"But there was no raging lust and spontaneous passion, was there, Caroline," he stated. "And though you had a lovely time, there was something missing."

"You don't know anything about it," she snapped, pulling her wrap around her more tightly, as if it could offer some protection from the truth.

"Then why don't you tell me. I've seen my share of marriages on the skids. Tell me. Why did your marriage break up?" he asked.

"It's none of your business," she replied, stalking away.

Tru watched her retreat. "Oh, but it is my business," he murmured, admiring the gentle sway of her hips and the curve of her sweet little backside. Though he had decided that her legs were her most alluring feature, he now had cause to revise his opinion. Her behind was just about the best that he'd ever seen, bar none. Maybe he wasn't a leg man after all.

When he caught up to her in the circular driveway, she was standing ten feet from his car, her hands on her hips, her beautiful face incredulous, her anger and irritation at him forgotten. He stood beside her, arms crossed over his chest. Her gaze wandered from the hood ornament to the leather upholstery to the tail fins. "What is this?"

"A '57 Cadillac convertible. It's a classic. This car's been in the movies."

"I think we should take my car," Caroline said.

Tru studied her. "Why? A little too outrageous for the very prim and proper Dr. Leighton?"

She met his challenging gaze with one of her own. "Despite what you think, I do enjoy spontaneous moments on a fairly regular basis. It's just that the BMW is much . . . smaller. I'm just not sure we'd find a place to park this . . . boat."

"We'll take that chance. Come on, Caroline, live a little," he teased. "Have some fun. Take a walk on the wild side."

She narrowed her eyes and glared at him through feathery black lashes. Then she strode over to the passenger side and yanked open the door. He got to her just in time to help her into the car and close the door behind her. "You won't be sorry," he said, with a grin.

"I already am," she muttered.

They wound their way back down Laurel Canyon Boulevard as the sky darkened to a deep purple and the first stars began to appear. The warm wind blew soft and gentle through the open convertible, reminding Tru why he loved Los Angeles. While he kept one eye on the road, he kept the other on Caroline. She worried over the stubborn strands of hair that whipped at her cheeks and neck, trying hard to maintain her perfectly polished appearance.

By the time they turned onto Santa Monica Boulevard, she'd meticulously tucked the same strand behind her ear for the umpteenth time. At the next stoplight, Tru reached over and yanked at the perfect knot, sending hair pins and jeweled combs flying. She cried out as her shoulder-length hair tumbled down around her neck, only to be tossed about by the breeze.

She slapped at his hand. "What are you—"

He placed his finger on her lips. "Relax." He brushed her hair away from her cheek. "That's much better."

"I look like a mess, thanks to you."

"The T.V. boys will love it. Trust me. I think I know men a little better than you do. And those guys will love the way you look right now. You look sexy and very feminine. And irresistible."

She grabbed the rearview mirror and twisted it toward her. "I do not!" She stared at her reflection. "You really think so?"

He pulled the mirror back in place and flipped her sun visor down to reveal another mirror. "Yes, I do. Now quit fishing for compliments from your husband and let me drive."

They drove the rest of the way in silence, Tru watching her out of the corner of his eye. He noticed that the nearer they got to the hotel, the more her apprehension grew and the more she fooled with her hair. He pulled up in front of the exclusive Regent Beverly Wilshire Hotel and stopped the car. For all her calm confidence and steely resolve, he could tell that this was one occasion where she was uncharacteristically unsure of herself— and probably even more unsure of him. The parking valet helped her out of the car and she waited while Tru tossed him the keys and gave him strict parking instructions. When he finally stepped to her side and took her hand, she looked up at him and smiled uneasily.

"Everything will be fine," he said, smoothing a soft strand of hair from her face. "Don't worry."

"I'm not worried. Not much. Do you remember everything we talked about?"

"Yes," he assured her. "Just relax."

"I can't relax. I don't know how I ever thought we could pull this off. If we leave right now, we can—"

"We're not leaving, Caroline." He pulled her along toward the door, but she stopped him and looked up hesitantly.

"Thank you, Tru. I really appreciate you doing this."

He grinned and arched his brow. "No problem, sweetheart. Superhusband Lance Leighton is always happy to stand by his wife in times of crisis."

CAROLINE PEERED through the group of syndicate executives who surrounded her, looking for some sign of Tru. She found him standing near the buffet table, casually watching her and nursing a watered-down Scotch.

Tru had stood silently by her side through the first hour of the reception, nodding in agreement with everything she said and offering a few benign comments of his own. But as she had predicted, his appearance at the reception was purely a formality. Once the introductions were made, Lance was excluded from all the business conversations and was gradually left to fend for himself.

For the past hour, Tru and Ellis Stone's beautiful wife, Marianne, had been sharing an intimate conversation over champagne and caviar. But to Caroline's relief, he was alone now. Though Marianne appeared to be merely completing her social obligations as hostess, Caroline sensed something more in her motives, something . . . predatory.

She groaned inwardly. What could she be thinking? Was she actually jealous? The notion was absurd. Still, she couldn't help but feel a bit possessive. Lance was her husband and he had been spending an inordinate amount of time with another woman. And a gorgeous one at that—tall, slender, blond, looks that oozed money.

Marianne crossed the room and joined Ellis in the group surrounding Caroline. She felt the woman's eyes bore into her, as if Marianne were assessing her, sizing up an opponent. Caroline looked her way and smiled. Marianne returned the gesture with a dazzling but transparent smile of her own.

She had nothing to worry about, she told herself. Tru was just being polite. And she had to admit that the evening was going rather well. They hadn't been tossed out on their ears yet. Tru had made a convincing Lance—so far. But then, Tru did have a particular talent for charming the women of the world. The men might not be as easy.

Her gaze wandered back in Tru's direction. He smiled at her and she smiled back. A warm heat washed over her body, and she was almost certain that she was blushing. Dressed in a tux, Tru made a singularly sexy impression, a tantalizing combination of dashing sophistication and rakish mischief. His thick hair, usually rumpled, was combed neatly back, making his handsome features even more pronounced.

She ignored the flush creeping over her cheeks and stared at him for a long moment, hoping that he might read her gaze as a sign for him to rescue her from this particular interrogation. Ellis and the executives surrounding her all seemed to be focused on her opinions on extramarital affairs. She felt as if she were on trial, as if they were weighing her answers against some predetermined set of entertainment criteria.

Though she hated to admit it, right now, she needed him. When he was beside her, his palm resting in the small of her back, she felt a distinct boost in her confidence. Part of it had to do with the fact that she didn't have to worry about what he was saying to someone else, but mostly it was because he seemed to truly believe they could pull this off. Caroline gripped her empty champagne flute. Though Tru hadn't a doubt in the world, Caroline's stomach was still tied in knots and the champagne she had gulped down earlier was making her nauseous.

"What makes men cheat on their wives?" Ellis asked.

Caroline smiled indulgently. "Research has proved that women tend to value monogamy, but men place less value on fidelity," she explained. "This male behavior has a basis in genetics—the more offspring to add to the tribe, the more success of survival. But we don't live in the Stone Age now, do we, gentlemen? Women today want a faithful spouse. And men have to subvert their genetic imprinting and learn to live in the twentieth century.

Many men choose to remain faithful, rather than risk the loss of someone they truly love."

"What about women who cheat on their husbands?" Marianne asked.

Caroline turned to catch a smug smile cross Marianne's lips. "Women?" she asked.

"Yes. After all, what's good for the gander is good for the goose. Isn't that how the saying goes?"

"If you're implying that mutual infidelity is good for a marriage, it's not," Caroline replied. "Most women cheat because their relationship with their husband is lacking in some area. Usually in affection or companionship or romance. It's important to communicate with your spouse, let him know your needs and desires, so that he can be a fulfilling mate. And your husbands must do the same."

She looked around the group and realized she had failed the test. They all looked positively bored, and a few of them even yawned. Though her answer was textbook perfect, it wasn't vintage Carly Lovelace. It wasn't audacious or humorous or even mildly entertaining. The knot in her stomach twisted another half turn and she forced a smile.

"If you all would excuse me," she murmured, "I need to check in with my service. I'll be right back."

Caroline slipped out of the room, but rather than head for the pay phones in the hotel lobby, she took a detour into the ladies' room. The elegant bathroom was empty. She closed herself inside a stall and sat down, then opened her purse and pulled out a neatly folded piece of paper. She quickly reviewed the list of goals she had made for the evening, trying to focus her mind on the task at hand. What was wrong with her? She had been worrying over this reception ever since she'd made the deal with Tru. But Tru was breezing through the evening with flying colors and she was making a total mess of the entire affair.

The sound of the door opening brought her upright and she tried to calm herself. Now was not the time for cowardice and capitulation. Now was the time to summon Carly Lovelace, that clever and entertaining queen of the evening airwaves. That's what these television executives wanted, not the cool and conservative Dr. Caroline Leighton. "You can do this," she repeated silently to herself. "You can do—"

"Lord, if I have to attend one more of these tedious business soirees, I'm going to scream." Caroline recognized Marianne Stone's voice immediately. She moved to step out of the stall, then decided to wait just a moment longer.

"Ellis seems to be enjoying himself," another voice said. "He's fawning all over that little doctor."

"Please, don't remind me," Marianne replied acerbically. "If there's a lovely, young thing within five feet of him, Ellis will always find a way to enjoy himself . . . and her as well."

"Do you think she's the one?"

"Maybe," Marianne replied. "I would have thought he preferred them with a little bit more air between the ears. That way they're not a threat to his inflated opinion of his intelligence. Still, she is . . . attractive, in her own rather intellectual way."

Caroline slowly sat down again, pulled her feet up and held her breath. Marianne couldn't actually believe that Caroline was having an affair with her husband! Ellis had never made a single move in that direction, and Caroline certainly hadn't either. He had been a perfect gentlemen since the moment they had met. Though she detested the fact that she was eavesdropping, she strained to hear more.

"Ellis is very, very careful about his affairs," Marianne continued. "Just because I haven't caught him yet, doesn't mean he's not cheating. I'm sure he'll mess up sooner or later and I'll finally have to confront him. Daddy is livid, of course. He wants me to divorce Ellis. But being married to the man does have certain . . . advantages."

"I can see at least one," her companion replied. "He introduced you to Lance Leighton. You seemed to be having a fine time occupying that gorgeous young man."

Marianne sighed dramatically. "He does fill out that tux, doesn't he? But what else could I do? His wife has practically deserted him. And he is too charming to be a wallflower."

"Poor thing. His wife works all day and night, and he stays at home writing some boring screenplay. So do you think he might be available for a little diversion?"

Caroline felt a healthy measure of jealousy shoot through her. She had been right! Marianne Stone was after Tru . . . No, not Tru. Her husband . . . No, not really her husband, her *make-believe* husband.

Marianne chuckled. "If I don't miss my guess, yes. That marriage is definitely in trouble. Believe me, darling, I know all the signs. Dr. Leighton can't even look her husband straight in the eye. And every time he touches her, she freezes. Ellis is prepared to dump my money into this harebrained project. A stuffy little radio marriage counselor who can't even keep her own man happy. Just imagine the ratings. It truly boggles the mind," she said, her voice filled with sarcasm.

The voices grew distant as Caroline heard the door of the ladies' room open and then swing closed. She released her pent-up breath in one long whoosh that turned to a moan. She should have known they couldn't pretend to be husband and wife, especially after just one morning together. Marianne had seen right through their act and in the process had set her sights on Caroline's husband.

Maybe it would be best to just collect Lance and leave, before the whole charade blew up in her face. She ran her fingers through her hair and sighed. No, she wouldn't give up—not yet.

Shoring up her confidence, she stood and smoothed her dress. There was still one way to salvage the evening. It was now or never. If she wanted this job, she'd have to quash all doubts about her talent—and her marriage.

When Caroline stepped back into the room, she found Tru in the midst of the group that included Ellis and Marianne Stone and a number of other executives and their spouses. She watched him from the doorway. He almost looked at home, smiling and nodding, so sure of himself. If only she had half his confidence, she wouldn't be in this ridiculous mess.

She drew a deep breath and walked over to the group. "Lance, darling," Caroline cried. "I'm glad you decided to join us." She wrapped her arm around his, then reached out and stroked her palm across his cheek. She risked a look at Marianne Stone, then stood on her tiptoes and gave him a kiss for good measure. "Are you having a nice time?" she asked.

Tru pulled back and stared at her as if she'd just sprouted horns and a tail. "Yes," he replied, a suspicious note creeping into his voice. "Are you having a nice time . . . dear?"

Caroline hugged him close and turned to the group. "I'm so lucky to have such a sensitive husband," she gushed. "Always concerned about my feelings. Most men feel a need to dominate in social situations, but not my Lance. He's very understanding. We have a very balanced relationship. Don't we, darling?"

"Yeah...sure," Tru said. "Balanced. Very balanced."

"Come on," Marianne teased, placing her hand on Tru's other sleeve. "You must fight about something. No marriage is perfect." She shot Ellis a malevolent look before turning her smile back on Tru.

Tru laughed. "Oh, we fight all right—"

"But only about inconsequential things," Caroline interrupted. "Lance always sees both sides of the situation and we work out a compromise."

Tru glanced around the group. "But not all the time," he said. "Sometimes, I'm right."

Caroline laughed lightly. "Isn't he sweet? Yes, sometimes you *think* you're right, dear. But that really doesn't make a difference, does it?"

Tru frowned. "It doesn't? I mean, no, it doesn't," Tru said uneasily. "No difference. None at all."

"No, of course not. You see," Caroline explained, "assigning blame and worrying about who's right and wrong is very counterproductive to a solid relationship. In fact, we had a small difference of opinion on our way here tonight, didn't we, darling?"

"Which difference of opinion was that?" Tru asked.

"You remember," Caroline said, hanging affectionately on his arm.

"Why don't you tell the story, Caroline?" he replied in a deceptively even voice. "You can tell it much better than I can."

"Actually, we got lost," Caroline began. "And all you women know how men are about asking directions. I'll never figure out why this country insisted on sending three men to the moon. Heaven knows, if they would have gotten lost, not one of them would have been sensible enough to ask for directions. Why, for all we know, they would have been circling Jupiter before they decided to find a filling station and ask for help. That's why they put women on the Space Shuttle, you know. It would have been awfully embarrassing to lose that, now, wouldn't it?"

The women in the group broke out in laughter and knowing nods. Marianne just smiled coldly.

"Didn't I tell you?" Ellis cried. "Isn't she funny? Women love her! She'll deliver our demographics on a silver platter."

"Right along with her husband, Lance," Tru muttered under his breath, just loud enough for Caroline to hear. "All sliced and diced and with his bones ready to be picked clean."

Caroline slanted a glance over at Tru. But his face was a mask, his emotions hidden behind a benign facade and a lukewarm smile.

"Well, I think we're ready to take the next step, don't you, gentlemen?" Ellis said. "What do you say we give Dr. Lovelace a chance in front of a real live audience? We'll put together a program, tape it, and your distribution experts can show it around and get a reaction from the market."

The syndicate executives glanced at each other for an excruciatingly long moment, then they all gave their enthusiastic assent. A wave of relief washed over Caroline as her hand withstood a barrage of handshakes. She'd done it! Dr. Carly Lovelace had passed the first test.

After everyone had congratulated her, Ellis grabbed her and kissed her cheek. "Well done," he said. "You had me worried there for a second, but the Dr. Lovelace we all know and love finally showed up." He bent over her ear. "Please make sure she shows up on the day we tape our pilot, will you?" he whispered, a desperate note in his voice.

She stiffened slightly and he loosened his hold. "I—I will," she said. "Don't worry." A wave of doubt washed over her. She'd managed to summon Carly Lovelace this time, but could she do it when it was really necessary, when she was standing in front of a television camera with an audience watching her? Caroline nervously looked over Ellis's shoulder to find Marianne Stone studying her like a hawk, a smug expression on her face. She'd never find herself in front of a camera if she didn't take care of more immediate problems.

Caroline turned to Tru. "Well, we did it, darling," she said, avoiding his piercing stare. Then suddenly, impulsively, she threw her arms around his neck. An instant later, she found her mouth pressed to his. She wasn't sure what made her kiss him, whether it was Marianne's watchful stare, or her own gratitude and excitement, or temporary insanity. But once she had started, she couldn't seem to stop.

His lips were firm and warm and she felt them part as he deepened the kiss. She wanted to pull away, knowing that they were being watched, but at that moment, every shred of willpower had somehow slipped from her fingers. His tongue touched hers and she felt a jolt of electricity shoot through her, numbing her nerves until her knees went wobbly and her head began to spin. This couldn't be happening. She had to stop him before she lost all her faculties. With great effort, she pulled away.

Tru looked down at her and smiled, his gaze clouded with what she hoped was confusion, but what appeared to be growing desire. "That was an interesting twist in the performance," he whispered. "But I think we need a little more rehearsal, don't you?"

If it weren't for the crowd standing around them, she was certain he would have mobilized a full-scale assault on her weak defenses. He wanted to kiss her again, hard and long. She could see it in his eyes. But she detected so much more than just a simple kiss there.

Her gaze darted around the room. Though the others were involved in more hand shaking and backslapping, Marianne Stone still watched them. Her expression of suspicion had been replaced by one that resembled envy. *Just try to take my husband away from me, Caroline* thought. As if Marianne could read Caroline's mind, she turned to her own husband and joined in his celebration.

"Are we through here?" Tru murmured. "Because if we are, I have a little matter of marital protocol I'd like to discuss with you. In private." Ignoring the others, Tru clasped Caroline's elbow and gently pulled her from the group, then headed her toward a small alcove that hid the entrance to the kitchen.

"Wha—Where are we going?" Caroline tried to pull out of his grasp, but Tru held tight. "Tru, stop it. We can't just leave. Let go of me."

"We need to talk," Tru said in a tight voice. "Now."

"About what? Everything is fine. We did it."

He pulled her into the alcove, then braced his arms on either side of her body and trapped her against the wall. "Would you like to explain what happened in there, Caroline?"

"I'm sorry, but I had no choice. I overheard Marianne Stone in the ladies' room and she suspected that we might be having marital problems, so I decided I'd have to . . . to . . . prove her wrong."

"So you made Lance look like a fool in front of everyone?"

"No! I kissed you! I decided it would be the only way for her to see that we were still passionately in love."

"I'm not talking about the kiss, I'm talking about the way you practically emasculated me out there. Caroline, every man in the room looked at me like I was some henpecked half-wit who lets his wife wear the pants in the family!"

"Don't be ridiculous. I did nothing of the kind," Caroline scoffed. "Besides, I was talking about Lance, not you. A person would have to be crazy to think you'd ever relinquish your pants to any woman, much less your wife."

"You made me look like a dope on a rope. They all pity me. They think I'm a wimp."

"They do not. They think you're a kind, sensitive man who only wants to make his marriage the best that it can be."

"They think I'm a wimp," he repeated.

"You're not—"

Her words were stopped short as he covered her mouth with his. The kiss was quick but thorough, sending a flood of sensation from her lips to the tips of her limbs. His hands cupped her face and as he pulled back, he looked deeply into her wide eyes.

"No, I'm not Lance and I'm not a wimp. The name's Tru Hallihan. And don't you forget that, Dr. Leighton."

With that, he turned and walked back into the reception room.

Caroline leaned against the wall and closed her eyes. He was right, she had to admit. Tru Hallihan was definitely not a wimp. And she wasn't about to forget it.

# 4

FIVE MINUTES after kissing Caroline, Tru watched her return to the room, her composure regained. He was deep in a discussion about fishing with Ellis Stone. For a two-timing slimeball who cheated on his wife, he really wasn't a bad guy. He wasn't much older than Tru, maybe forty tops, and had grown up not far from Tru's old neighborhood in Reseda. For a lower middle-class kid from L.A., Stone had done quite well for himself, though it obviously hadn't hurt to marry money.

Ignoring their conversation, Caroline walked right up to him, a determined look in her eyes. "Darling, I think it's time to say our goodbyes," she ordered. "You have to catch an early plane tomorrow."

"You're going out of town?" Ellis asked.

Tru looked to Caroline. This was her story, not his. She was responsible for the details, even if they did contradict his.

She nodded. "Yes, Ellis. Lance is going to New York... on business. He'll be gone for a long, long time."

Ellis turned back to Tru. "But you'll be back by next weekend, right? We're looking forward to having you spend some time at our place up at Lake Arrowhead."

"Lake Arrowhead?" Caroline asked.

Tru smiled. "Ellis offered us the use of his vacation home at Lake Arrowhead for next weekend, darling."

Caroline smoothly contained her surprise, replacing it with a bland expression. "And you told him you'd still be in New York, didn't you, dear?"

"No. In fact, I'll be back by then. I accepted the invitation for us both."

"You—You accepted?" she gasped. "But Lance, I'm sure you're not scheduled to come back from New York until long after the weekend. Don't you remember? We discussed this earlier."

Tru shook his head. "No, Caroline, I'm sure I'm coming back on Thursday. Besides, I'm looking forward to a quiet weekend in the mountains. Ellis says the fishing is terrific. We'll have a wonderful time."

"I don't think so, Lance."

Lord, the woman could be stubborn. But he wasn't about to play the yes-dear-whatever-you-want wimp, again. It was time for Lance to stand up to his domineering wife like a real man. Tru tried to keep his voice calm and even. "Caroline, I want to accept Ellis's invitation. We *are* going to accept his invitation and we are going to Lake Arrowhead. End of discussion."

Ellis clapped him on the shoulder, clearly proud of Lance's first foray into self-assertion. "Well, there it is!" Ellis said. "Lance, here's my card. Give my secretary a call and she'll give you directions and the code for the security system. The key is under the clay pot next to the door of the toolshed. I want you two to have a nice, quiet weekend. After Caroline's show gets underway, you'll have little time to spend together. Take it while you can."

Tru held out his hand and Ellis shook it. "Ellis, thank you. I'm looking forward to a little fishing and lots of relaxation. And I'm sure Caroline will enjoy herself, as well. Won't you...dear?"

Ellis turned to Caroline and she smiled uneasily. "Yes. Of course," she replied. "Thank you, Ellis. Now, I think Lance and I had better be going. I'll call you with my ideas for the first show."

Caroline grabbed Tru by the arm and they worked their way through the room, her anger evident only by the fingers digging into his forearm. Once they exited the room, she was silent, her eyes fixed straight ahead, her temper simmering just under the surface. She didn't speak until he'd pulled the car out onto Wilshire Boulevard.

"How could you?" she cried.

Tru frowned. "How could I what?"

"How could you accept another invitation from Ellis Stone?"

"Gee, I'm not sure," Tru replied. "The guy offers me a free weekend at a luxurious mountain retreat. I haven't been out of the city for months. Never mind the fact that he doesn't take no for an answer. You should know that."

"And you know this wasn't part of our deal. Lance is supposed to disappear after tonight. You know he's not an outdoorsman!"

"He's a guy, Caroline, and guys like fishing. It's in the genes. Besides, how do you know what he likes? He doesn't even exist."

"He doesn't like fishing and he doesn't like the mountains," she insisted. "I know that!"

"Geez, what would you have him do for fun? Needle-point and gourmet cooking? I happen to like the outdoors."

"What you like doesn't matter. You're not my husband."

"You're acting like this is my fault."

"Well, whose fault is it?"

"Assigning blame and worrying about who's right and wrong is very counterproductive to a solid relationship," he mocked. "Now, where did I hear that?"

"We don't have a relationship!"

"You kissed me," he said.

"So? You kissed me."

"And you liked it, didn't you?"

She glared at him, her dark hair flying across her face. "I didn't like it a bit." She looked wild and reckless and he was tempted to pull the car over to the curb and kiss her again. She had the most delectable mouth he'd ever seen, even when it was pouting in that stubborn way of hers. He definitely liked Caroline Leighton's mouth. Even better than he liked her legs. Or her backside.

Slouching down in the seat, she pulled her wrap around her and crossed her arms over her breasts. She looked like she was ready to punch him in the nose. Either that, or jump out of the car and find another way home. God, she was magnificent when she was mad. Her ice-cool attitude disappeared and she seethed with fire and passion.

The rest of the drive passed in silence. As Tru pulled into her driveway and stopped the car, he wondered whether he had been dreaming to think the evening would end any other way than with them at complete odds. He'd never met a woman quite as contrary as Caroline Leighton. No wonder her husband took a powder. A man would have to have a will of iron to stand up to her domineering day after day.

Caroline pushed the door open and got out, then slammed it behind her. "Goodnight, Mr. Hallihan. And goodbye. Since you didn't fulfill your half of the bargain, I'm not going to fulfill mine," she said. "Don't hold

your poker game up waiting for me. I'm not coming."
She turned and started up the driveway.

Tru cursed softly then hopped out of the car without
opening the door. "Wait just a minute. I did everything
I was supposed to do. They believed I was your husband. And you got what you wanted."

She spun around and faced him. "And you accepted
that stupid invitation to Stone's vacation home. Don't
bother canceling, I'll do it for you. Lance is about to go
on a very extended business trip."

"You make that call and I'll make one of my own. I'll
tell Ellis Stone all about our long and happy marriage. It
won't take much time to explain the last three days!"

She glared at him, her eyes glinting with carefully
controlled fury, her fists clenched. "Just as I thought! You
are capable of blackmail. You are nothing but a disreputable sleaze—"

Tru grabbed her arm and pulled her against him, then
lowered his head and kissed her. She didn't fight him. She
seemed too stunned to offer any resistance and by the
time she realized what was happening, the kiss had gone
way beyond just simple contact. No matter how hard she
tried, he knew she couldn't deny that there was something between them. She couldn't ignore the heat that
they generated. When she went soft in his arms, he pulled
away and looked down into her wide eyes.

She took a deep but shaky breath. "—ball, a slimy
bastard who wouldn't know the meaning of the word
honor." She continued on, as if his kiss merited no more
notice than a buzzing mosquito. "I wish I'd never made
this deal. I'd have been better off making a deal with the
dev—"

He pulled her into his arms again, this time determined to prove his point. His mouth came down on hers,

cutting off her tirade in midsentence. His tongue played at her lips, teasing and taunting until she opened beneath him. A tiny moan escaped her and he smiled inwardly. He drew away again and looked down at her flushed features and swollen lips. His thumb traced a line from her moist mouth to her defiant chin.

"You can kiss me all you want," she murmured. "I'm not going to change my mind about you or Lake Arrowhead."

"But it's sure fun trying, isn't it?" he said with a grin.

She scowled at him, almost daring him to try again. But beneath her stubborn expression, he could tell that her resistance was faltering.

"All right," she said, yanking out of his grasp. "Just how much was the stupid bet worth?"

Tru shrugged. "Around one hundred fifty dollars."

"One hundred fifty dollars," she muttered as she fumbled through her purse. She pulled out a pen and her checkbook, then scribbled a check and tore it out. "A pittance. Well worth it to get you out of my life." She shoved the check at him. "Here, take it. That should clear us."

He bent toward her to kiss her again and she stepped back, then shoved the check in his jacket pocket.

"You've done your job and you've done it well. And now, there's no reason for us to ever see each other again. Goodbye, Mr. Hallihan." She spun around and stalked up the driveway.

"This check doesn't square our deal, Caroline," he called. "I'll expect you at Flynn's on Tuesday night."

"Don't hold your breath," she called back.

"YOU SHOULD HAVE COME with me," Aurora gloated, as she dumped her shopping bags on Caroline's desk.

"There's a certain benefit to shopping with a psychic, you know. I can sense where all the great buys are. Look at these," she said. A pair of olive green combat boots thumped down, nearly upsetting Caroline's take-out salad and iced tea.

"Lovely," Caroline said. "When are you leaving for psychic boot camp?"

"You have no sense of style," Aurora teased. She pulled out a pair of black metal-studded pumps with four-inch heels.

"Interesting," Caroline commented. "And were they running fifty percent off matching whips, too?"

"I did find something for you," Aurora said. She pulled out another shoe box and opened it, then withdrew a pair of taupe pumps and waggled them in front of Caroline's nose. "Two inch heels, seven B in a neutral color. Fifty-six dollars, originally one-twenty."

Caroline snatched them from her. "Aurora, these are lovely! I've been looking for a pair in this exact shade with a low heel. They're on the top of my wardrobe list. How did you ever know I needed these? And how did you know my size?"

Aurora smiled smugly and tapped her temple with a fuchsia-tipped finger. "Psychic," she said. "And you showed me your list the last time we went shopping."

"Thank you," Caroline said. "These will match my new suit perfectly."

Aurora flopped down in a guest chair and threw one leg over the arm. "You know, I can tell a whole lot about a person by her shoes. Forgive the pun, but they're like a window to the soul. Sometimes they work better than tarot cards."

Caroline groaned at the silly joke. Whenever she felt down, Aurora could always pick up her spirits and make her smile. With her crazy hairstyles and outlandish clothes, Aurora approached life at full throttle, determined to wring every ounce of energy out of it. And though she seemed perpetually distracted by the world around her, Aurora could sense when Caroline's mind was in disarray and she'd drop by for a heart-to-heart.

"Though Freud might have ignored shoes as an analysis tool," Caroline replied, "I'm open-minded. Tell me your theory. What do you see in my soles?"

Aurora picked up a taupe pump and examined it. "These shoes are definitely you. The minute I saw them, they cried out your name. Well, they didn't actually cry out loud, but they did speak to me telepathically."

"And what did they say?" Caroline asked. "Did you have a full-fledged conversation or just a quick chat?"

"They told me that for the most part, this is who you are to the world—neutral, conservative, practical." She picked up the black pump with the four-inch heel, then placed it beside the taupe. "But sometimes, this is who you'd like to be—bold, uninhibited, and a little bit reckless."

"I would not! I wouldn't be caught dead in those shoes," Caroline cried.

"But Carly Lovelace would," Aurora replied. "And isn't Carly Lovelace just the real you trying to get out?"

Caroline opened her mouth, then snapped it shut again. She had to admit, the sexy shoes did hold a certain fascination for her. From the minute she saw them, she wondered what they might look like on her feet. Though she had never considered *herself* the slightest bit reckless or uninhibited, Carly Lovelace certainly was. And maybe Carly was just an easy way to enjoy the wilder side of her psyche.

A year ago, she would never have considered a man like Tru Hallihan attractive. He was the ultimate bad boy, the kind she warned her radio audience against. The kind she was determined to rehabilitate into proper mates. But now, she found herself inexplicably drawn to him. And though she knew he was trouble, she couldn't seem to get the scoundrel out of her mind.

"Go ahead," Aurora urged. "Try them on. I know you want to."

Caroline looked over at her friend's amused expression. Aurora did have a surprising talent for reading her thoughts. Surprising and very annoying at times.

"All right! But only because I know you'll never let it go if I don't." Caroline kicked off her sturdy navy pumps and slipped into the black shoes. "There, are you satisfied?"

"Dat ees not da question here, Dr. Leighton," Aurora said in an exaggerated Freudian accent. "How do zose shoes make *you* feel?"

"Ridiculous," she grumbled. "And maybe a little uninhibited," she admitted. "All right, I feel positively reckless."

Aurora giggled in satisfaction. "Some women need years of hundred-dollar-an-hour therapy to find their inner self and Aurora Starr does it with a pair of shoes." She watched as Caroline took a few turns around the room. "Those shoes were made to make a man beg for mercy. They should be registered as dangerous weapons. Darrell would love them. They'd drive him wild with desire."

Caroline smiled. It was hard to imagine Darrell going wild over anything. On the surface, he and Aurora were the two most mismatched people in the world. He was painfully shy and soft-spoken, and worked as a computer programmer for one of the country's largest video game manufacturers. He and Aurora had been "two halves of the same whole" for nearly fifteen years. That was the only explanation Aurora offered for the longevity of their marriage, though Caroline had often pressed her for more.

In the course of Caroline's work she rarely came across a marriage that hadn't lost its luster. But Aurora and Darrell had found some magic to keep their marriage alive and vital. Caroline wished she could bottle whatever they had and prescribe it to her patients. It would certainly make her job much easier.

"How do you do it?" Caroline asked distractedly as she strolled around her office, staring at the shoes.

"It's all a matter of balance," Aurora explained. "That and watching out for the cracks in the sidewalk. Just keep your weight on the balls of your feet."

Caroline stopped. "The balls of my feet? What does that have to do with a successful marriage?"

Aurora frowned. "I thought you wanted to know how to walk in those shoes."

"This is crazy," she muttered, shaking her head. She flopped down in her chair and kicked off the shoes.

"You want to know how Darrell and I have kept our marriage together?" Aurora asked.

Caroline nodded.

Aurora took a deep breath and considered the question for a long moment before answering. She smiled. "Well, it's all a matter of balance. That and watching out for the cracks in the sidewalk. And—"

"Keeping your weight on the balls of your feet," Caroline finished.

"That's really about all there is to it. It's not as complicated as it would seem. There's just never been any doubt in our minds that we were meant to spend our lives as husband and wife. And all the problems we have seem to be pretty insignificant when you compare them to the cosmic forces that brought us together."

"But you and Darrell are so different," Caroline said.

"Sometimes I think that's what makes it work. Darrell still continues to fascinate me. He's everything I'm not and I'm everything he's not. Every day is an adventure."

Strange. That's how she'd have to describe Tru and herself. "But it's not that simple, Aurora. I've tried to put hundreds of marriages back together, and there's much more involved."

"I think a relationship is what you make it. If you want to complicate it with lots of preconceived notions and elaborate expectations, then it will be much harder to make it work and it will probably self-destruct. Keep it simple and pure, focus on the feelings."

*Keep it simple and pure.* Years of education, a Ph.D. in psychology, and a prestigious Beverly Hills practice and Aurora's words made more sense then anything she'd ever read or heard. Suddenly she felt very tired. Tired of trying to keep couples together who never really loved each other in the first place. Caroline sighed. "That's the problem with marriage today. People expect too much. Including me."

"So what's really bothering you, Caroline? You didn't ask me here to talk about my views on marriage."

"I didn't ask you here at all. You just dropped by."

Aurora shot her a dubious look. "All right, if that's what you want to believe. Now, why don't you tell me all about him."

"Him?" Caroline gasped. "Who?"

"The man who's occupying your thoughts. I'm picking up some strange vibrations. I see your husband, but not Edward. You might as well tell me, Caro, because you know I'll get it out of you sooner or later."

"I'm going to fire Janine," Caroline threatened. "Just as soon as I find someone who can do her job as well as she does."

"Janine didn't say anything to me."

Caroline searched her desk for her fork and began to pick at her salad, trying to appear indifferent. "His name is Tru Hallihan and he's a private investigator. He's also Lance Lovelace and he's my husband."

"You found someone to pretend to be Lance?"

"Yes. And he did a good job. The producers think I'm happily married and they've given the go-ahead to tape a pilot show. After that's over, I'll tell them the truth."

"Then what's the problem?"

"There's no problem. In return for his appearance, I'm supposed to go to his poker game tonight. I mean Dr. Carly Lovelace is supposed to go. But I'm not going."

"Why not?" she asked. "It sounds like fun."

"I don't want to go. Tru Hallihan drives me crazy. He makes me do and say things that—that—Aurora, I'm a well-respected psychologist and I can't for the life of me figure out why he gets to me like this. Besides, he didn't exactly keep his side of our bargain, so I don't think I should have to keep mine."

"What are you afraid of Caroline?"

"I'm certainly not afraid of him! But when I'm around him I feel...out of control, like all the Ph.D.s in the world won't help me. I'm an expert in human behavior, I can predict human response, even direct it in many cases. That's my job."

"But when he kisses you, all your self-control flies out the window, right?"

She sighed and threw her fork down into her salad. "Yes, that's exactly it. I'm attracted to him, though God knows why. I know he's trouble. He's definitely not my type. He'd make a horrible husband."

"You sound just like one of your radio listeners. So Dr. Carly Lovelace, what would you advise Caroline Leighton to do?"

"I'd tell Caroline to trust her instincts and stay as far away from the man as possible. Move to another state, another country, and find a man who's made for marriage."

Aurora stood up and snapped her fingers. "There's your answer then."

"So, that's what you think I should do?"

"No, that's what Dr. Lovelace thinks you should do. I think there are cosmic forces at work here, Caro. It's no use running away from destiny. I'd advise you to listen to your heart and keep an open mind."

"So you can continue reading it?"

"The phone book has been more interesting of late," Aurora teased as she walked to the door. "But I'm beginning to think there might be hope for you yet."

Aurora had already swept out before Caroline realized that she'd left the black spike heel shoes beneath her desk. She quickly gathered them up and ran after her. "Aurora, you left your shoes!"

Aurora stopped at the door to Caroline's suite and turned around, a conspiratorial smile curving her lips. "I didn't buy those shoes for me, Caro, I bought them for you. Besides, they're not my size." With that, she waved and walked away, her bracelets jangling all the way across the atrium.

Caroline glanced down at the black leather and shiny studs, then looked over to Janine. Her receptionist raised a skeptical brow.

"They're you," Janine said. "Definitely you."

"I DIDN'T COME HERE to be interrogated about my date," Tru said. "I came here to play poker."

"You had a date?" Josh asked. "When was this?"

"You were here, Josh, remember? Last Saturday night? The tux?"

Josh frowned. "I thought Garrett said you were going to a funeral."

Tru smiled and shook his head, then shuffled the cards. Leave it to Josh. If the conversation didn't include a high level of mathematical reasoning, Josh was usually tuned out in favor of the all-accounting channel. But if the talk turned to investments, tax loopholes, and the general state of the Internal Revenue Service, Josh was at the center of the discussion.

"So, how *was* your date?" Garrett asked.

"Who said I had a date?"

Josh looked at him, bewildered. "You did. Just a minute ago."

Tru shrugged. "It wasn't really a date, it was a social obligation. Merely an exchange of services."

"A barter?" Josh asked.

Tru nodded.

"You know, the tax ramifications of bartering goods or services is quite complex," he said, as if thinking out loud. "One party is required to claim the barter as an expense and the other as income. It's also required that you fill out a Form 1099 for the—"

"Don't worry, Josh," Tru interrupted. "I don't think this particular exchange falls under the jurisdiction of the IRS."

Bob and Eddie returned from the bar, where they had gone to get another round of beer, and Garrett began to deal the next hand.

"Five card draw. So how's your case going?" Garrett asked. "Have you caught the guy with his pants down yet?"

"No, not yet. But I'm getting closer. A lot closer." Tru sat back in his chair and stared at his cards, trying to erase the eerie sense of fate that seemed to hang over him like a cloud of smog on a sunny day. How much easier could it get? He had met both Ellis and Marianne Stone less than three days before. He had a personal invitation to their damn vacation home! And from what he already knew of Ellis, all it would take to get the goods would be a few dry martinis and some indiscriminate locker-room conversation.

Tru sucked in a long breath. Why was he so uneasy about this case? The twenty-thousand was nearly his for the taking. But he had the overwhelming feeling that there were other forces at work here. The meeting with Simon Marshall and the offer of work, right out of the blue and right when he needed it the most. And then the odd coincidence with Carly and Caroline, the voice on the radio and the face through the telephoto lens. Her relationship with Ellis and his with her. And, of course, the mirror...

"If you're so close, why do you look so grim?" Garrett asked. "I thought this case was worth big bucks."

Tru glanced up. "It is," he said. "If I prove grounds." He hesitated. "McCabe, you know how this town works. I've got a hypothetical situation—"

"Does it involve twins and a hot tub? Hypothetical situations can be so much fun."

"No, this one involves a production company. The husband runs it, the wife bankrolls it. The wealthy father-in-law suspects the guy of cheating and wants the son-in-law out of the family for good. What happens to the production company?"

Garrett smiled. "Ellis Stone is cheating on his wife?"

Tru raised a brow. There were times that Garrett's inside knowledge amazed him. "No. This is purely hypothetical. Besides, even if I knew who you were talking about—and I'm not saying I do—there is such a thing as client confidentiality."

"Well, hypothetically speaking, I'm not a divorce lawyer," Garrett said.

"But if the company was formed after their marriage, it's community property," Josh stated. "She'd own half. Since the money comes from the wife's premarital bank account, I'd assume she'd relinquish or sell her share of the business and refuse to invest another cent . . . at least that's what I'd advise her to do."

"And the projects that the company is working on would . . ."

"Fall through," Garrett completed. "He doesn't have much capital of his own. He'd have to rely heavily on investors, but without some of his own money in the mix, I don't think he'll have many takers. Does that answer all your questions?"

"Yeah, it does." Tru turned his attention back to the game, but he couldn't ignore the irony of the situation. Over the past three days, he found himself thinking of Caroline more than he had wanted to—her sexy voice, her gorgeous legs and that sweet mouth of hers. An image of her strayed in and out of his mind so many times that he had given up trying to fight it, and instead decided to enjoy it. After all, it helped pass the endless hours of surveillance work.

It wasn't as if he held any responsibility for Caroline's happiness. Simply thinking about the woman certainly didn't constitute a relationship. Yet, through some misguided sense of honor, he felt a compulsion to give the job up. He knew what this opportunity meant to Caroline and he was reluctant to cause her any pain.

But he also knew what this case would mean to him. Twenty thousand and a regular paycheck. A chance for a solid future for his business. No more living from referral to referral, doing without electricity and a car until the next case came along.

He glanced at his watch. Ten-thirty. She was late...very late. Her show was over at nine and the drive was only forty-five minutes at the most. His gaze swept the bar and lingered at the door. Had he really expected her to show up? After all, she'd paid him off to avoid seeing him again and they hadn't parted on friendly terms.

"Well, Hallihan, where is she?" Garrett asked, reading Tru's thoughts.

"Where is who?" Josh asked.

"Dr. Carly Lovelace," Bob said. "Tru was supposed to bring her to our poker game."

Tru tossed three chips into the pot. "I'll see you and raise you five."

"I remember the bet involved boxer shorts," Garrett prodded. "And beer, wasn't it? So, where is she?"

"She'll be here," he muttered. "Don't worry."

"You found out who Dr. Carly Lovelace really is?" Eddie asked.

"Yep," Tru replied. "She's a marriage counselor named Caroline Leighton. She has a practice in Beverly Hills."

"At least show us the black-and-white glossies," Garrett said.

"She broke my camera," Tru said, smiling at the memory of her indignant reaction.

"Come on, Tru," Eddie said. "She's not really coming here, right? I can't wait much longer. Kim is going to kill me if I don't get home soon."

"Ah, the joys of marriage," Garrett teased. He held his hand above his head and yanked it up, as if pulling a noose tight.

"It's not all that bad," Eddie said. "You really ought to try it."

"Not in a million years," Garrett replied. "Some of us are meant to live the good life, right, Tru?"

Tru shrugged. "I don't know. Marriage might not be so bad, if you find the right woman."

"Give me a break!" Garrett cried. "What's wrong with you, Tru? Did you get into another brawl with one of your disreputable clients? Did someone hit you over the head? Or maybe Dr. Lovelace brainwashed you. You can't actually be changing your views on marriage. Josh, do you hear what Hallihan is saying?"

"There are certain tax advantages to marriage," Josh stated. "And once a married couple has children, the benefits increase greatly."

"I wouldn't mind finding a woman and settling down," Bob added. "Did Dr. Lovelace offer you any advice on finding a wife, Tru?"

"I can't believe what I'm hearing," Garrett said. "Have you guys lost your minds?"

"I like being married," Eddie said. "Kim and I have a solid relationship and we've got our baby girl, Sharon.

And it's nice to have someone who believes in me. I hate the fact that she makes more than I do, that she supports the family, but she never throws it back in my face. She has complete faith in me, which is more than I can say about myself sometimes."

"And it really doesn't cause a problem that she makes more than you do?" Tru asked.

"It won't be that way forever," Eddie replied. "If I could sell my script, I could contribute a little more."

"Well, you can contribute twenty-five dollars more this week," Garrett said. "I don't think Dr. Lovelace will be joining us tonight."

"That wasn't the bet," Josh said. "Tru had to identify her and bring black-and-white photographs. Since he found out who she is we should at least pay him some of the money."

"Never mind, Josh," Tru said. "I concede the bet. You guys can keep your money as long as I don't have to walk through Flynn's in my shorts." Tru tossed his cards on the table and gulped down the rest of his beer. "I'm done for the night. I've got an early day tomorrow."

Tru stood up and walked toward the door. That's when he saw her, standing near the bar. He watched as she leaned over to speak to the bartender. The bartender pointed in the direction of the back room and she turned, her gaze meeting his.

He watched her spine stiffen and her expression freeze. She strode toward his table, nodding at him as she passed, a manila envelope clutched in her hand. Tru turned in time to see her stop at the poker table. The guys put their cards down and looked up at her with curiosity.

"Gentlemen," she said. "My name is Dr. Carly Lovelace." She opened up the envelope and withdrew a stack of black-and-white photos, then walked around the table, efficiently placing one in front of each of the four gawking poker players. "I understand Mr. Hallihan promised you photos. I hope these will be satisfactory. Now, I believe that completes Mr. Hallihan's part of the bet. Good night."

As quickly as she had blown in, she blew back out again, an Arctic hurricane, leaving only an icy silence in her wake.

Garrett scowled as he watched her retreat. "*That's* Dr. Carly Lovelace?"

"It sure sounded like her," Eddie commented.

"That was definitely Dr. Carly Lovelace," Tru said. "I'll see you guys later. And don't forget, you each owe me twenty-five dollars," he called as he ran to the door.

She was halfway to her car by the time he caught up to her. "Caroline, wait a second." He grabbed her elbow. She stopped but refused to turn around.

"Come on, Caroline. This is no way to treat your husband."

She shook her head and chuckled softly. "If I'd have known you'd be so hard to get rid of, I never would have married you."

"You don't really want to get rid of me, do you?" he said.

She turned and faced him, a rueful smile touching her lips. "I don't need a husband anymore. And I don't think you want a wife."

"How do you know what I want?" Tru asked.

She drew a deep breath and clasped her hands in front of her, twisting her fingers nervously. "Tru, I think it would be best if we called a permanent end to this . . . arrangement of ours. Take it from someone who knows the delicate dynamics of male-female relationships. We should count ourselves very lucky that we weren't really married. It would have been a disaster of epic proportions."

"It wouldn't have been that bad," he teased.

Caroline opened her purse and pulled out a piece of paper. "Here, look at this. I made a list of all the reasons we should avoid a relationship. And then, on the back, I made a list of all the qualities that I'm looking for in a man."

Tru examined the lists, written in her tidy, precise hand. "More lists," he murmured.

"Tru, I really appreciate what you did for me, and I hope I squared our deal tonight. *And* I hope you understand why this has to be the end of it."

Tru sighed and nodded, then handed her the paper. "Yeah, I understand. But we're not quite square on our deal," he said, reaching into his back pocket for his wallet. He withdrew the check she had scribbled out for him that night in her driveway. He tore it in half and pressed it into her hand. "Now we're square."

"Goodbye, Tru," she said.

"Bye, Caroline." He watched her walk away, tempted to call her back. But instead, he mentally reconstructed the lists she had shown him. She was probably right. The reasons that she had written down made perfect sense. They were from different planets when it came to relationships with the opposite sex. Still, he couldn't help but think that whatever had begun to develop between them shouldn't simply be reduced to one of her lists.

As the taillights of her BMW faded into the night, Tru shrugged off the vague sense of regret. He drew a deep breath and shook his head. So much for untapped potential.

Studying the list, Tru slowly walked the short distance to his apartment, his mind still swimming with an image of Dr. Leighton. The apartment was dark when he walked in. He headed for the stereo, flipping it on to fill the empty silence. But the quiet jazz didn't satisfy his need for sound and he pushed the Play button on the cassette recorder. Her voice came to him, as if in a dream, a repeat of her show from earlier that evening. He threw himself on the couch, closed his eyes and listened.

*"And now, back to 'Making Your Marriage Work' with Dr. Carly Lovelace."*

*"Good evening, Los Angeles. Last night we talked about my 'Six Steps to Marital Success.' Before we close for the evening, I'd like to just review them for a moment. I think you'll find that if you keep these particular items in the forefront of your relationship, you'll find that your marriage will become stronger and more vital every day. Communication is the cornerstone of any successful marriage. Compatibility and caring are the two elements that brought you together and will keep you together. Compromise and candor will help you over those rough spots. And finally, there's commitment, the element that holds all of this together. Those are the six C's for a successful marriage and this is Dr. Carly Lovelace. Join us tomorrow night on KTRL for 'Making Your Marriage Work.' Good night."*

Commitment. He had never placed much credence in the concept. It was easy to say the words, to act out the concept, and still never believe in the meaning. But it was even easier to walk away, as his mother had so many years before. He remembered how his father, an L.A. cop, had simply wandered through life after she'd left, taking little pleasure in anything that reminded him of her—including his nine-year-old son. So Tru lost himself in books, detective novels, stories of clever, independent men who trusted no one and had no use for commitment.

Tru had often thought about tracking his mother down and finding out why she'd left. But he really didn't need to know. He'd inherited one thing from her—a restless spirit—and that alone explained a lot. He hadn't had a real relationship with a woman since graduate school. There had been women since then, but they had never occupied a place in his life, or in his heart. One day they were there, and the next, they were gone. No responsibility, no regrets, and nothing to distract him.

So why was Caroline Leighton plaguing his thoughts? It wasn't as if he had developed any real feelings for her. They had been involved in a simple deal and now it was through. He'd never see her again. They'd go on with their lives as if they'd never met and he'd prove grounds on the Marshall case and take his business right to the top.

A stab of guilt pierced his conscience and Tru swore silently. Why should he feel guilty? There was nothing between them. She had put an end to any contact they might be tempted to have. Hell, he couldn't care less what Caroline thought of him. She was out of his life. For good.

Still, he couldn't shake the feeling that he was damned if he made the case and damned if he didn't. "That's the whole problem when a guy lets a woman into his life," Tru muttered, throwing his arm over his eyes. "There's no way to win."

# 5

THE LATE-AFTERNOON light shimmered across the surface of Lake Arrowhead, dancing and shifting with each breeze that skittered over the water. Caroline sat at the end of the pier and gazed out at the peaceful scene, the autumn wind caressing her face and teasing at her loose hair. Her bare toes skimmed the water as she swung her legs lazily back and forth.

She'd left Los Angeles early that afternoon, fighting bumper-to-bumper Friday traffic on the San Bernadino Freeway. Her nerves and her patience had been shot when the exit for State Highway 18 appeared. The urban sprawl of San Bernadino soon disappeared as colorless concrete and steel were replaced by the blue-green and gray of the chaparral and rock landscape in the foothills of the San Bernadino Mountains.

Near the tiny town of Crestline, the highway intersected with a road called the Rim of the World Drive. The mountain scenery that followed had been breathtaking, filled with stunning vistas and awesome landscapes, a startling contrast to the wall-to-wall civilization she'd left behind. A half hour later, she had opened the back door to Ellis Stone's "little" home away from home. Or more appropriately, his mansion away from mansion.

A weekend in the mountains hadn't appealed to her at all when Ellis had first offered, especially when faced with the prospect of spending it "married" to Tru Hallihan. She'd called Ellis on Thursday, simply to make sure that Lance had canceled their weekend, which he had, to her great relief. But by the time the phone conversation was over, Ellis had convinced *her* to make the trip to Lake Arrowhead—alone.

She had hesitated at first, but then gave in, knowing that Ellis rarely took no for an answer. Besides, she needed a weekend away, a quiet time to put her brief "marriage" to Tru out of her mind for good. Time to get over her inappropriate infatuation with the man. Time to stop waiting for him to call and time to rid herself of the temptation to call him. She'd leave her problems behind in L.A. and when she returned, they'd all be gone, forgotten.

At least, that's what she hoped. But Tru Hallihan was a difficult problem to leave behind. Since they had parted for good on the street in front of Flynn's, thoughts of him had tormented her every waking hour. And woven through it all was a pervading sense of regret. Though she knew Tru could only be trouble, she couldn't help but wonder whether that trouble might well be worth it.

She'd never been as sexually attracted to a man as she had been to Tru. Even Edward didn't possess the kind of masculine magnetism that Tru did. Her marriage to Edward had seemed more like a professional partnership than a passionate alliance. She had known her husband so well that it had been impossible for him to surprise her with either word or action. But somehow, she knew it would take a woman a lifetime to plumb the depths of Tru Hallihan's psyche. And in that prospect, there was a certain fascination. Life with Tru would never be dull, that was certain.

Caroline sighed and ran her fingers through her windblown hair. The lap of the water against the pier numbed her jangled emotions and she concentrated on the soothing rhythm. "Life with Tru," she murmured, then laughed, the sound echoing across the gleaming water. It was almost an oxymoron. Tru and commitment stood at opposite ends of the relationship spectrum. There wasn't a chance in a million that she could expect a normal relationship with him. He wasn't the husband type. And deep in her heart, she wanted to try marriage again. She wanted a second chance to make it work, to correct the mistakes she'd made the first time, to find a man made for marriage.

"The only way to put Tru Hallihan out of your mind is to stop thinking about him," she muttered to herself.

She turned and looked back at the house, shading her eyes from the sinking sun. Ellis Stone's vacation home was built on an extraordinary piece of property. The house stood above the lake on a gentle rise, a wall of glass and a huge deck facing the water. Thick trees separated it from the other homes. From where she sat, the only evidence of neighbors were the piers that jutted out into the lake at regular intervals.

Such a romantic hideaway, she thought. A perfect spot for an intimate rendezvous. Caroline ground her teeth at the capricious thought. She wasn't going to let the lack of a male companion spoil her weekend. She didn't need a man to be happy. *No* man was certainly better than the *wrong* man, she assured herself, repeating one of her top ten radio proverbs. And Tru Hallihan was the wrong man! How many times would she have to remind herself of that fact before she actually believed it?

She stood up and grabbed her shoes, then started up the steps to the house. It was nearly dinnertime and she hadn't bothered to check the refrigerator when she came in. A trip into the village for groceries was probably the next item on her vacation agenda and she began to compile a grocery list in her mind as she walked through the door and into the house.

As Caroline turned the corner into the kitchen, she stopped short. A man stood at the refrigerator, his backside and legs the only part of his anatomy visible from behind the open refrigerator door. She froze, unable to decide whether the man actually belonged in the house or whether he was just a hungry burglar. Suddenly, he stood up and slammed the refrigerator door.

Stifling a tiny scream, Caroline jumped back and spun around, determined to make it out of the house before she found out just what the stranger wanted.

"Caroline?"

She skidded to a stop at the familiar voice, then slowly turned and walked back into the kitchen. "Ellis? What are you doing here?"

He smiled in his typical charming way. "I own the place."

Her hand fluttered to her chest and she felt her heart thudding beneath her fingers. "You nearly scared me to death."

"I'm sorry. I rang the bell but there was no answer. I figured you went out for a walk. I just stopped by to see how you were doing."

"I'm doing fine," Caroline said. "Or I will be once the fright wears off."

"I'm sorry," he repeated. "I was just checking the refrigerator. I see the market in town stocked it." He frowned. "I'm going to have to discuss their selection of wines with them," he said, distracted. "They have a tendency to send out a few questionable vintages whenever given the opportunity."

"You drove all the way up here to see if the refrigerator was properly stocked?"

He shifted his attention back to her. "Of course not. I brought you some research data on talk shows I thought you might be interested in reading." He stepped over to the counter and pulled a stack of file folders from his briefcase. "I've got a barbecue to attend across the lake and thought I'd stop by on the way. You are all right here by yourself, aren't you?"

"Of course," she replied. "I—I'm having a wonderful time. The house is beautiful, the lake is beautiful. It's all . . . beautiful."

He studied her for a long moment. "Caroline, stop me if I'm interfering, but is everything all right—I mean, between you and Lance. Are you two having . . . problems?"

"No . . . no, wherever would you get an idea like that?" She forced a bright smile. "We're very happy, very . . ." She drew a deep breath and struggled to find an appropriate word. " . . . happy. Really."

He regarded her candidly, as if weighing the truth of her words, then nodded. "Good. I'm glad to hear that at least someone I know has a good marriage. I guess a marriage counselor would know how to keep her own relationship on an even keel."

"Yes, she would. *I* would. My marriage is on the *evenest* keel a woman could want."

Ellis rubbed his palms together and smiled. "Well, I'd better be going." He walked toward the door, then turned back to her. "If you don't have any plans for dinner, you're welcome to join me. Max and Arlene Winter always put on a terrific barbecue."

"Isn't Marianne with you?"

His expression tightened at the mention of his wife's name. "No, she hates these business obligations. She stayed in Bel Air. I believe it was a headache this time."

"Well, I'm ready to settle in for the evening myself," Caroline said. "I'm anxious to read the research you brought and I'll have a chance to work on my outline for the first show."

Ellis smiled dryly. "That's much more important than some boring barbecue with a bunch of show business types. I'll call you early next week and we'll set up a meeting to discuss your ideas. Have a nice weekend, Caroline."

"I will, Ellis. And thank you—for the weekend and for your concern."

Caroline followed him to the door and locked it behind him. So his wife had stayed behind. Her mind wandered back to Marianne's stinging ladies' room commentary on her husband. Was Ellis really involved in an extramarital affair? She knew infidelity wasn't an uncommon occurrence in Hollywood; her clients were living proof.

But there was something about Ellis and infidelity that didn't quite mix. She'd seen it in his eyes when she mentioned Marianne's absence. It wasn't anger or bitterness or vindictiveness. It seemed more like sadness and regret, genuine pain, as if he'd given up on something he believed in.

Maybe he had. The money for Stone Productions came from Marianne's bank account. Marianne and her father suspected Ellis of cheating. If there were a divorce, Ellis would probably lose everything. And Caroline's show would join the hundreds of other promising concepts that never made it out of development. Ellis's career would be gone in a snap of Marianne's perfectly manicured fingers.

Caroline sighed. A wife who wielded that kind of power made marriage difficult at best, and the male ego wasn't indestructible, no matter what most women believed. All the signs pointed to the imminent end of Ellis and Marianne's marriage. What could she do, except stand by and watch it unravel in front of her, her dreams right along with it? She wasn't a television producer, she knew nothing about putting together a television talk show, or even how to find someone else who could.

She rested her forehead on the cool glass of the door, her gaze following Ellis's car as it pulled out of the driveway. "All I know how to do is save marriages," she said to herself. Save marriages. A smile tugged on the corners of her mouth. Wasn't that all she really needed to do? Save Ellis and Marianne's marriage. In the process, she'd save her television show.

Caroline spun away from the door and clapped her hands. She could do it, she knew she could! Ellis and Marianne were no different from any other couple that she'd helped. They were still married, so there must be at least a glimmer of hope alive in both of them. And many marriages had weathered infidelity, or suspected infidelity. Her "Six Steps to Marital Success" would be put to the most difficult test yet.

As she walked back into the kitchen, her mind spinning with the possibilities, Caroline noticed Ellis's briefcase on the counter. Good! He'd probably come back for it or at least stop on his return to the city. Maybe she'd broach the subject of counseling then. And if he didn't stop in, she'd take the briefcase with her when she went back and call him upon her return. It would give her the perfect excuse to see him immediately.

Caroline glanced around the kitchen then walked over to the refrigerator and peeked inside. True to Ellis's word, she wouldn't have to worry about food for the weekend. The fridge was stuffed with enough variety to please any gourmet. She pulled out a bottle of wine, uncorked it, and poured herself a celebratory glass. Things had definitely taken a turn for the better.

As she sipped her wine, Caroline wandered through the huge house, snooping inside closets and touring each room. The master bedroom was incredible, boasting a stunning view of the lake and a bathroom built for the pages of *House Beautiful*. She opened the French doors that led out to the deck overlooking the lake. There, nestled up against the house and made perfectly private by the surrounding trees and the encroaching night, was a huge whirlpool spa.

She pulled the cover back and dipped her hand into the hot water. Ellis did think of everything. A long soak in a hot tub sounded like the perfect prelude to a quiet and leisurely dinner and an evening spent reading Ellis's research. After a brief flicker of modesty and a careful evaluation of her privacy, she stripped off her jeans, her loose cotton shirt and her underwear, and tossed them in a pile next to the tub. Caroline Leighton might not be brave enough to skinny-dip, but Carly Lovelace certainly was!

Gingerly, she stepped into the water then sank down into it until the liquid warmth reached her neck. She felt reckless, decadent, and just a little bit naughty. She turned the jets to the lowest setting, then leaned her head back and stared up into the midnight blue sky as the water bubbled around her naked body. As the outside temperature dropped, the steam rose from the tub until she could barely see her hand in front of her face. The wine, the long drive from L.A., the soothing rumble from the tub, all combined to make her drowsy. Her eyelids fluttered closed and she let her mind and body drift. This was pure bliss.

He came to her in the hazy world between wakefulness and sleep. Like a phantom lover, he materialized from the mist, standing over her, a strange unearthly light gleaming off his naked chest. His gaze captured hers and she saw desire burning deeply in his hooded eyes. He knelt down beside her and gently reached out to brush a bead of perspiration from her temple. Slowly, she pushed up from the water, arcing her neck against the rim of the tub. He sat back on his heels and waited until the water sluiced from her breasts in a brazen invitation, her moist, heated flesh exposed to his eyes and his touch. He bent over one nipple and with exquisitely slow and deliberate movements, he touched it with his—

She woke up with a start. For a moment, she didn't know where she was. The sky was black and filled with twinkling stars. She reached over and turned off the whirlpool jets and listened carefully. The air was quiet, the soft breeze rustling the tall pines the only sound she heard. She sank back into the warm water and closed her eyes, hoping to resume the delicious dream where she had left off, but a sound from inside the house brought her fully awake. Footsteps. Her heart leapt to her throat, choking off a cry of alarm. She had locked the door. It had to be Ellis, she assured herself, returning for his briefcase. Her panic subsided.

"Ellis?" she called. "Is that you?"

In the next instant, a tall form appeared in the French doors, outlined by the light from the master bedroom. She froze. An eerie sense of déjà vu washed over her as her mind tried in vain to juxtapose her dream with reality. She instinctively sank down into the water up to her chin. "Ellis?"

"I thought I recognized that voice," the man murmured. She watched through the steam as he approached the hot tub, making out long legs clad in jeans, a T-shirt stretched tight over a muscular chest, and a rumpled linen jacket. Her gaze moved to his face and she let out a scream that echoed through the trees and across the lake.

Tru Hallihan gave her a sexy grin as he took in the scene. "Is that any way to greet your husband, darling?"

THE UNDERWATER LIGHT in the tub filtered through the still water, outlining every delectable curve of Caroline's naked body. Tru's gaze drifted from her damp shoulders to her perfect breasts, just visible beneath the surface of the water. He was about to delve a little lower when she realized what he was staring at.

"Get out!" she screamed, scrambling to turn the jets back on and conceal her nakedness. She cranked the jets up to maximum and the water bubbled furiously, hiding her delicious body. Slowly, he approached the tub. Her green eyes widened with his every step. He took a seat on the edge and watched her in amusement as she crossed her arms over her breasts.

"How's the water?" he asked, dipping his fingers into the roiling tub.

"Just deep enough to drown you in," she hissed.

He smiled, then bent down and picked up her clothes. One by one, he bunched each item into a ball and tossed it across the deck, saving her panties for last. He dangled those on his finger in front of her. She glared at him mutinously, refusing to reach out and grab them. With a sigh, he tossed them in the direction of her other clothes. "He shoots, he scores," Tru cried. "And the crowd goes wild."

"You are slime. No, you're lower than slime, you're sludge."

"Name-calling is not going to get you out of the predicament you're in," he teased.

"You are despicable," she said through clenched teeth. "What are you doing here?"

Tru wasn't about to tell her the truth, that he had come up to the cabin hoping to discover Ellis and one of his paramours in bed together. He'd called Stone Productions on Monday to get the directions to the lake house, still planning to take the trip. He called on Wednesday to cancel, after Caroline had showed up at the poker game. By then he was ready to put the woman and their "marriage" well in the past.

The time on either side was spent tailing Ellis Stone all over L.A. But either the man was very cagey about his extramarital affairs or he wasn't engaging in that sort of pleasure. Earlier that afternoon, he'd followed Ellis Stone right out of Los Angeles and west on the San Bernadino Freeway. He'd lost him in a rush hour traffic jam, but he had known exactly where Ellis was headed. He was headed for Lake Arrowhead.

Still, the last person he expected to find at the lake was Caroline. The house had looked deserted when he arrived, until he saw her white BMW parked in front of the garage. He had knocked but there had been no answer, so he disarmed the security system and jimmied the door. The rumble from the whirlpool tub had drawn him out onto the deck where he'd found her, naked, in Ellis Stone's hot tub. Waiting for . . . for Ellis.

He crossed his arms over his chest, carefully controlling the thread of distrust that wound around his heart. "What am *I* doing here? I could ask you the same question. In fact, I am. What are *you* doing here, darling?"

Her mouth tightened and her chin tilted up defiantly.

"You're not going to answer me?" He stretched his legs out and braced his arms behind him. "I'm willing to wait. You can't spend the rest of your life in that tub. The shrivel factor will get to you sooner or later."

Tru watched her gaze dart back and forth between him and the French doors, as if she were waiting for something—or someone. Either Ellis hadn't arrived yet, or he had stepped out for a moment. But Caroline definitely was expecting him. Dammit, she had called out his name! Wasn't that all the proof he needed?

Jealousy knifed through him at the thought of Caroline tempting Ellis from the hot tub, as she was tempting him now . . . of Ellis joining her in the bubbling water, as he wanted to do himself. He had blithely written off the possibility of an affair between the two of them, but maybe he'd been too hasty. Maybe he had only *wanted* to believe there was nothing between them. Maybe that was what *she* wanted him to believe.

If there *was* something going on between the two of them, Ellis certainly wouldn't expect to encounter a jealous "husband" when he returned. No, Tru wasn't about to leave. This weekend promised to be very interesting, with or without Ellis Stone. And the hot tub was looking more inviting by the minute.

"You aren't supposed to be here," Caroline said petulantly. "You canceled just like you were supposed to do. We had a deal."

"I changed my mind," he said with a shrug. "When I got here, the key wasn't where it was supposed to be, so I had to break in. Imagine my surprise when I found you here. Alone. And . . . without a stitch." He stood up beside the tub and pulled off his jacket, tossing it in the direction of her clothes.

"I want you to leave," she demanded, pounding her fists on the rim of the tub.

His eyes wandered down her slick chest to the rosy tips of her breasts, just breaking the surface of the water. She realized what he was staring at and, with an astonished cry, slid back down into the water.

He ignored a tightening in his groin and bent down to tug off his shoes and socks. "I'm not going anywhere, Caroline. I've been driving all afternoon through rush hour traffic and I'm not about to turn around and drive back to L.A. So cut me some slack, all right?" With that, he pulled his T-shirt over his head and dropped it at his feet. The night air was cool, raising goose bumps over the length of his torso. Her gaze fixed on his naked chest and she chewed nervously on her lower lip. He moved to unbutton his jeans and she winced.

"Stop it!" she cried. "You're not getting in this tub with me!"

He flipped open the top button and grinned. "The way I see it, there's not much you can do to stop me. Unless, of course, you'd like to get out of the tub."

She groaned and slapped the water with her palms, sending a shower of droplets falling over him. "Why are you here?" she cried. "I came up here to get away from—" she swallowed hard "— for a nice, quiet weekend. I'm not going to let you spoil it. Just go away and leave me alone."

He stretched his arms above his head and worked a few kinks out of his back, covertly watching her gaze skim along his chest and belly and stop at the top button of his jeans. She stared long and hard, her brow furrowed slightly, as if she were trying to figure out what the next open button might reveal.

Tru rubbed his chest distractedly and her eyes followed every movement of his hands. "You know what I need?" he asked softly.

She shook her head.

He stretched again. "Um. I need a beer."

"Wh-what?" she croaked.

"I need a beer. Is there any beer around here?"

"Th-there's beer in the refrigerator," she said, suddenly anxious to be helpful. "In the kitchen. That's inside the house."

He grinned, then turned and sauntered through the French doors, stopping just inside. The sound of water sloshing turbulently and muttered feminine cursing drifted in from the deck. He was tempted to turn around and catch her scampering naked to collect her clothes. But he was certain that one look at her sweet body would definitely be his undoing. It would be impossible to keep his hands off Caroline after that. If his guess was right, she was his twenty-thousand-dollar lady, and he wasn't about to do anything to jeopardize his prize.

He strolled into the kitchen and yanked open the refrigerator door, then pulled out an imported beer and the makings for a ham sandwich. As he folded a slice of meat into a piece of bread, he glanced up to see Caroline storm into the room, her white shirt clinging to her damp skin until it was nearly transparent. In her haste to dress, she hadn't bothered with her bra.

"I have to admit, I was surprised to find you here," he commented, before biting into his sandwich. Her nipples puckered against the wet cotton, tantalizing him until his fingers itched to touch her there and his mouth craved the taste. He forced back a rush of desire that threatened to make him instantly hard and swallowed convulsively, forgetting to chew first. "I—I thought you didn't like the great outdoors. Or were you and Ellis planning to spend your weekend indoors?"

His gaze lingered for a long moment on her breasts. He had compared the relative attractiveness of her legs, her backside and her mouth, but now he had cause to revise his earlier opinions. Her breasts were definitely her most appealing feature. He glanced up to find her frowning at him.

"What is that supposed to mean? Ellis isn't staying here."

The lump of ham sandwich lodged in his throat and he coughed. "Funny," he choked out. "I could have sworn you were expecting him." A look of utter confusion crossed her face and his heart twisted. Maybe he *had* been wrong. He cleared his throat. Or maybe it was just the ham sandwich going down the wrong way.

"I was," she replied.

He clenched his teeth and held his temper, his fingers making mush of the sandwich.

"He stopped by earlier and forgot his briefcase," she continued. "I thought he had come back to pick it up. What does Ellis have to do with your being here?"

Tru eased his punishing grip on his meal and placed the wad of bread and meat on the counter in front of him. Suddenly, he wanted to know the truth. He didn't want to figure it out on his own, or see it through a telephoto lens, he wanted to hear it straight from Caroline's perfect mouth. He looked deep into her green eyes and she met his gaze rebelliously. "Are you having an affair with him?" he asked.

She blinked once, then gasped. "What?"

"You heard what I said. Are you having an affair with Ellis Stone? Is that why you needed a husband for the reception? To deflect suspicion? Or were you trying to fool

Marianne into believing there was nothing going on. Or maybe it was to make him . . . jealous?"

She shook her head and laughed harshly. "You are insane. Certifiably cuckoo. I must have been crazy to ever get involved with you."

"So, you're not having an affair with Ellis Stone?"

"No! But whether or not I'm having an affair with Ellis Stone is none of your business. We made a deal, a business deal, and now that deal is complete. I want you out of my life!"

Tru grinned and took a long swallow of his beer, satisfied that he had his answer. She wasn't Ellis Stone's mistress. The fact didn't make him any richer and for that, he expected to feel at least a little disappointed. But strangely enough, he didn't feel that way at all. He felt relief, satisfaction, and something akin to happiness. "I'm not *in* your life."

"Oh, no? You're acting just like a jealous husband. Following me up here to check up on me. Accusing me of cheating on you. You're—you're obsessed!"

Tru flinched slightly. Over the past few days, he'd often suspected as much. Still, it stung hearing it from her. "No way," he said coolly. "Not even close, sweetheart."

"Then why *did* you come up here?"

"I didn't even know you'd be here," Tru replied, dodging the truth. "I came up for some peace and quiet. For some fishing and a free weekend. And now I'm stuck with you and Mr. Showbiz."

"You can always leave," Caroline suggested.

"And leave you here alone with Casanova?"

"Casa— Ellis is not staying here with me. Can't you get that through that thick caveman skull of yours?"

"I think I'll stick around and see for myself. A man's got to protect what's his."

"What's his?" she cried. Her temper flared and the color rose in her cheeks. He waited for the verbal on-slaught, but this time, she reined in her indignation. "Fine," she snapped. "Suit yourself. Stay as long as you like, but stay away from me. I don't want to see you or hear you for the rest of the weekend. Got that?"

"No seeing, no hearing. Got it." He paused and grinned. "Does that mean touching is out, too? How about tasting?"

She screamed in frustration, slamming her clenched fists against her thighs, then spun around and stalked through the living room, a string of vividly worded as-persions on his character left in her wake. She flung open the French doors that led onto the deck and stamped through them.

Tru grabbed his beer and stood in the open doorway as he watched Caroline make her way down to the pier. She plopped down at the end of the dock and stared out at the lake, her slender form illuminated by the yellow light at the end of the pier. She looked so vulnerable, so alone. A fierce surge of protectiveness overcame him and he suddenly regretted pricking her temper. He didn't re-ally want Caroline angry at him. He just couldn't figure out how they always ended up that way.

Tru stepped out onto the deck and retrieved his T-shirt, then tugged it on. He snatched up his jacket and slung it over his shoulder, then jogged down the steps that led from the deck to the lake. He approached her slowly, his bare feet nearly silent on the wooden pier. He stood over her and she shivered, as if she sensed his presence. Bend-ing down, he placed his jacket over her shoulders. "It's getting chilly out here."

She didn't answer him. He sat down beside her and stared out at the twinkling lights across the lake. "I was thinking that maybe we could renegotiate our deal," he said.

She turned to him, one side of her face limned golden by the light on the pier, the other deep in shadow. "Our deal is over," she said. "Done. Complete. There's nothing left to renegotiate."

"All right, then maybe we could strike a new deal."

"Why would I want to do that?"

He paused. "Well, I think we get along pretty well and I was—"

"Tru!" she cried. "We don't get along at all! We are the most mutually incompatible pair of human beings on the face of this planet. We're always fighting."

He paused to consider her statement. "All right," he admitted. "Maybe we don't exactly get along." He grabbed her hand, warming her icy fingers between his palms. "But I do like you."

"I don't like you," she said stubbornly.

"Yes, you do. I can tell. Come on, Caroline, admit it. You like me. At least a little bit."

She fought a smile, but the corner of her mouth turned up. "All right. Maybe I like you a little bit. Sometimes. When you're not driving me crazy."

"Well, there, that's a beginning."

She smiled forlornly. "It also can be an end. Tru, it takes a lot more than just liking each other to make a relationship work."

He wove each of her fingers through his, distracted by the delicate bones of her hands, the soft, smooth skin and her tiny wrist. "A relationship? I wasn't talking about a relationship, I was talking about a few dates, maybe dinner and a movie, or we could go to a Raiders game."

"See, there it is. You want dinner and a movie. I want a relationship. You want football, I want commitment."

"With me?" he asked.

"No, not necessarily. But with someone. Someone who's compatible with me. Someone who wants the same things from life as I do."

Tru leaned over and brushed a kiss across her silken cheek. Her skin suddenly warmed beneath his lips and he could feel her blush, even if he couldn't see it in the dark. "We're compatible."

"No, we're not."

He turned and stared across the lake again, avoiding her gaze. "Is it because I don't make enough money?"

"No!" She clutched his upper arm and shook her head. Her hands felt good on him, warm and soothing, understanding. "That doesn't even appear on my list of top twenty reasons. Money has never been a motivating factor in my life. It goes much deeper than that. There are fundamental differences in the way we think, in what we want from life."

"How do you know how I think?"

"Believe me, I know. And I can prove it to you. We'll do a little test."

"This isn't going to be another one of your lists, is it?"

"No, this is a word association exercise. I'll give you a word and I want you to say the first thing that pops into your mind."

He nodded once. "All right, shoot."

She studied him carefully. "Up," she said.

"Down."

"Black."

"White," he replied. "This is supposed to show you how I think?"

"We're just practicing," she said.

"I think I've got the hang of it," Tru commented dryly. "Try something harder."

"All right. Happy."

"Birthday," he replied.

She slanted a questioning glance in his direction.

"Was that wrong?" he asked.

"No, there are no right or wrong answers in this test. How about this one—content."

"Burp."

"Burp?"

"Yeah. You know, after you have a big Thanksgiving meal and you settle down to watch a football game with the guys, and have a few beers. Burp. This is really easy, give me another one."

"All right. Close," she said.

"Call."

"Touch."

"Tone."

"Communication."

"Satellite. How am I doing?"

"I haven't decided yet. Trust."

"Fund. I thought you said money didn't make any difference."

"It doesn't. Candor."

"Camera."

She smiled. "Very funny. I want you to take this seriously. This isn't a game. Love."

"Umm, this *is* serious," he murmured.

"Answer me. Love."

"Me Tender."

She frowned. "Me tender?"

"My favorite Elvis song. 'Love Me Tender.' I like 'Jailhouse Rock' too, but I've always been partial to his ballads."

"Commit," she continued.

"A crime."

"Marriage."

"Divorce."

She stopped suddenly and turned her gaze back out to the lake.

"Is that it?" he asked.

"Yes," she replied, her voice soft and defeated. "That's it. The experiment is over. I rest my case. We have absolutely nothing in common." She struggled to her feet and slipped his jacket off her shoulders. "I'll see you in the morning."

He took his jacket from her outstretched hand. "Come on, Caroline. Stay a little longer. We'll forget the word association and just talk."

"I'm tired, Tru. You stay if you'd like, but I'm going to bed."

Tru stared out across the lake as he listened to her footsteps trace the length of the dock and fade into the night. An aching emptiness slowly settled into his gut and for the first time in his life, he felt lonely. He wanted to call her back and sit beside her just a little longer, to listen to her soft breathing and inhale the flowery scent of her hair. He wanted to hold her hand in his and feel her warmth seep into his fingers. He wanted to kiss her and taste her sweet mouth beneath his.

But she didn't want him. According to her, they weren't compatible and without compatibility the rest was impossible. She had devised a strict set of guidelines for the men in her life, a checklist for happiness, and right at the top of the list was her "Six Steps For a Successful Marriage." Hell, he hadn't even gotten past step one.

Tru kicked at the water in frustration, sending a plume of spray up into the night air. Maybe it was for the best. Caroline wanted something he could never give her. She wanted a commitment, a relationship, marriage. He pushed to his feet and drew a deep breath. He'd best forget about Caroline and get on with his life. He had a job to do. And once he proved Ellis Stone's infidelity, there wasn't a chance in a million that Caroline would want anything to do with him anyway. Tru headed for the house. Now was the perfect time to forget about Caroline and do a little snooping. And he'd start with Ellis Stone's briefcase.

By the time Tru finished copying all the women's names out of Ellis's address book, it was nearly ten o'clock. He replaced the book in the briefcase, then grabbed another beer from the refrigerator and stretched out on the couch. His mind wandered to the bedroom down the hall and he buried the urge to go to her, slip into her bed under the cover of night and make love to her.

Tru closed his eyes and imagined her lying naked, amid a tangle of sheets, craving his touch, her beautiful green eyes speaking her need, her perfect breasts cupped in his palms, her long legs wrapped around his waist. And he imagined that voice, whispering her pleasure, urging him on. He smiled at the notion of showing Caroline Leighton just how compatible they really were.

She came to him in the hazy world between wakefulness and sleep. Her warm mouth touched his, soft and moist, a fleeting caress. He moaned in response and then she was gone. He relaxed back into the dream and waited for more. A moment later, her hands splayed across his chest, then skimmed along his shoulders and down his arms. He could feel her weight against his body as she stretched out on top of him. Her mouth came down on his again, this time with more passion. His hands slid to her waist and he grabbed her and rolled her over beneath him on the couch.

"You're the very last person I expected to find here," she murmured against his ear.

Tru frowned and pinched his eyes more tightly closed. Something wasn't right. That voice. It didn't belong to Caroline. He reluctantly opened his eyes, wondering if the dream would evaporate upon waking. But it didn't. He blinked hard and found himself gazing into the smiling face of Marianne Stone.

"Whoa!" he shouted, pushing away from her and scrambling to his feet. He stood next to the couch, rubbing his hands against his jeans as if they were suddenly dirty. He wiped his wrist across his mouth and laughed uncomfortably. "And you're the last person I expected to . . . to . . ."

"Whom did you expect?" she said in a teasing voice. "Your wife?"

"Wh-what are you doing here?"

She laughed lightly and crawled off the couch, slowly stalking him. "The truth?" she purred.

He nodded and backed away, circling the couch.

"I came up here expecting to find my husband and one of his little bimbos."

He feigned a look of surprise, which wasn't hard to do. That's exactly why he had come. Tru groaned inwardly. He thought he had had a handle on this case, but throwing a horny Marianne into the mix complicated matters. "You think your husband is cheating on you?" he asked innocently. Simon Marshall had been so sure that his daughter didn't suspect her husband of infidelity. In fact, he had portrayed Marianne as a virtuous victim in this whole marital mess. It was blatantly clear that Marianne was far from sainthood.

"Oh, don't be shocked, darling. I know all about his little peccadilloes." She placed her perfectly manicured hand on Tru's chest and smiled. "In fact, I'll let you in on a little secret, if you promise not to get too angry at me."

"A secret?" Tru asked, stepping away from her touch.

"I expected to find my husband here... with your wife." Her hand reached for his face and he felt her fingernail skim his jawline. "You don't seem surprised, Lance."

Tru raised a brow. "Ah, right now, nothing would surprise me."

"Then you're glad to see me?" she murmured.

"Well, I—"

Suddenly, Marianne's arms snaked around his neck and she pushed him over the back of the couch. They tumbled into the cushions and she ended up straddling his waist. "I'm so glad you said that, Lance. I'm hot for you. Ever since we met, I've been thinking about how good we'd be together." She leaned over his chest and pressed her mouth to his, grinding her body and her lips against his.

He opened his mouth to protest and she stuck her tongue inside. On even the worst of days, he would have accepted Marianne's advances with hearty approval. After all, she was gorgeous. And she had money. A deadly combination. But this little tryst had a distinct air of sleaziness about it. *She* was married. And *his* "wife" was asleep in the other room.

"Marianne," he said, pushing against her shoulders as he pried his mouth from hers. "Come on. This isn't right."

She knocked his hands away and continued kissing him.

He tore his mouth from hers. "Marianne!" he shouted. "Stop this! I'm a married man."

"And I'm a married woman," she said, frantically unbuttoning her blouse. "See, we have something in common after all."

Tru opened his mouth to chastise her again, but his words were replaced with someone else's voice.

"Marianne!"

Tru pushed Marianne off of him and she rolled to the floor. He struggled to his feet only to find Ellis Stone standing in the doorway, a thunderous expression on his face.

"Ellis!" Marianne cried, scurrying to her feet next to Tru and buttoning her blouse.

"Tru!" Caroline's voice suddenly joined the chorus.

Tru spun around to find his "wife" standing on the opposite side of the room, her hair tousled and her eyes sleepy.

"Lance!" Tru reminded her.

"And Caroline!" Marianne cried. "Now that we've taken roll call, let the orgy begin."

# 6

TRU WATCHED as Caroline brushed the sleep from her eyes and stared at the scene unfolding before her. A blush stained her cheeks pink and she tugged nervously at the tie of her silk robe. She opened her mouth to speak, then obviously thought better of it, shaking her head in disbelief. Ellis, though outwardly cool, was trying hard to hide his shock and embarrassment. Marianne seemed to be delighting in the confusion, a hard smile curling her lips. She tossed her disheveled hair over her shoulder. The blond strands slapped him in the face and he winced.

"Maybe you'd like to tell me what you're doing here, Ellis?" she asked in a haughty tone.

"What *I'm* doing here?" Ellis inquired, clearly abashed by the question. "I walk in and catch you kissing Caroline's husband. What do you think *you're* doing?"

She licked her lips seductively and tugged at her rumpled clothes. "Nothing more than you had planned with your little friend over there. That is, until her husband showed up. I'm sorry to have missed your arrival, Lance. The last I'd heard, you'd canceled. It must have been quite a surprise for Ellis."

Tru ground his teeth. He'd suspected that Ellis was on the make, but now he had corroboration—from his own wife. "So, you *did* come up here to seduce Caroline!" he shouted. He turned and gave Caroline a satisfied smile. "See, I told you, Caroline. You can't trust this man."

Caroline gasped. "Don't be ridiculous! I told you, Ellis just dropped some papers off for me earlier, then went on to a party."

"I just dropped some papers off," Ellis reiterated.

"A likely story," Marianne said. "You didn't expect your tootsie's husband to show up, did you, Ellis?"

Caroline's temper flared at Marianne's patronizing attitude and Tru watched her work up a good case of righteous indignation. "I'm not his tootsie," she snapped. "And for your information, he's not my hus—"

"A likely story," Tru interrupted, shooting her a quelling glare. The last thing they needed now was to add more fuel to the inferno. Revealing the true state of their relationship would only make matters worse. "When I walked in earlier, you thought I was Ellis," Tru continued. "What's a *husband* supposed to think?"

Caroline swallowed hard. "I—I explained that," she replied, trying to cover her near mistake.

Marianne's arm snaked around Tru's and she smiled up at him, batting her lashes. "Darling, any woman can see, you're definitely not Ellis."

"Give it a rest, Marianne," Tru said, pulling out of her grasp.

"And who did you think Marianne was when you were kissing her, *Lance?*" Caroline asked.

"I'd like to know the answer to that question, too," Ellis said. "Who *did* you think my wife was?"

"I thought she was *my* wife!" Tru explained.

"A likely story," Caroline said. "You've never kissed me like that!"

"Maybe that's why he was enjoying himself so much," Marianne added smugly.

"He wasn't enjoying himself," Caroline cried. "And I'd appreciate it if you'd get your hands off my husband."

"Get your hands off her husband, Marianne," Ellis ordered.

Marianne held onto Tru's arm and smiled. "Only if you promise to keep your hands off his wife."

"I never put my hands on his wife," Ellis said.

"Neither have I!" Tru said.

"A likely story," Ellis growled.

"What I meant was, I've never put *my* hands on *your* wife," Tru explained, pulling out of Marianne's grasp. "Not intentionally."

Suddenly, the conversation lost all semblance of civility as Ellis and Marianne began to hurl accusations at each other. As the only qualified psychologist in the room, Caroline attempted to jump into the middle of it all and officiate, but it was impossible to get a word in edgewise. Tru decided to play it safe and stay out of the fray.

After trying in vain to calm the couple, Caroline glanced over at Tru for help. He shrugged, then turned back to the action. This was better than Friday night at the fights. He listened carefully to every blow that was landed, hoping for another bit of evidence to add to his case file, a name, an accusation, anything to put the poor couple out of their marital misery.

"Ellis, Marianne, please," Caroline pleaded in a calm voice. The fight raged on as if she hadn't spoken at all.

"I don't think they're listening," Tru said, walking across the room to stand beside her. "They're having too much fun tearing each other apart."

Caroline stuck her fingers in her mouth and whistled shrilly, a talent that seemed totally incongruous with her professional demeanor. "Ellis! Marianne! Stop your bickering this instant!" she screamed.

The quarreling ceased and the couple turned to gape at her, as if they'd just realized she was still in the room. "This type of behavior is unacceptable," Caroline stated in an authoritative tone. "Why don't we sit down and discuss this misunderstanding in a calm and rational manner? I'm sure we could—"

"And why don't you put a sock in it!" Marianne yelled. She grabbed her bag from the floor beside the couch and stalked off toward the bedrooms. A door slammed moments later.

"Ellis, I think it would be best if—"

"Not now, Caroline," he said harshly, then trailed after his wife. Another door slammed.

The sudden silence vibrated through the room and they stood for a long moment, staring after the combatants. "Now there's a marriage to admire," Tru muttered. "I wouldn't worry about dividing the family china and crystal in that divorce. By the time they get to court, it will all be broken."

Caroline glanced over at him and sighed. "What makes you so sure they'll divorce?"

He chuckled. "Oh, they will. Believe me, I can read the signs and they're all there."

Caroline walked over to the hallway and peered around the corner, then turned back to him. "And I suppose you're speaking from experience? The last time I checked, you were terminally single."

"You don't have to swallow arsenic to know it'll kill you."

"Marriage is not a fatal disease, Tru," she said with an exasperated frown. "With the proper preparation and effort, marriage can be a very satisfying facet of life."

"Right. Is that why you divorced your husband?" Tru asked. "Because your marriage was so satisfying?"

His blunt question startled her and he immediately wished he could take it back. "I didn't divorce my husband," she said softly, the pain in her voice carefully fashioned to sound like indifference. "He divorced me. I wanted to work out our problems, but he wasn't interested."

The misery and regret in her voice pierced his heart and sapped the breath from his lungs. Her tough, determined facade had dropped and she looked hurt and entirely vulnerable. He wanted to pull her into his arms and tell her that Edward had been a fool. He stepped toward her and she jumped back, avoiding his gaze and rubbing her arms as if she were suddenly cold.

"Do you still love him?" Tru asked.

Her head snapped up and she looked at him. "No! It took me a long time to come to terms with my failure to make our marriage work, but I finally realized I couldn't *make* Edward love me, no matter how hard I tried."

"Believe me, Caroline, you're not that hard to love. Maybe Edward was the one who failed you."

She smiled waveringly. "This from a man who thinks marriage is worse than a life sentence in San Quentin. I'll take that compliment with a grain of salt."

He placed his hands on her upper arms and gave her a squeeze. "Take it the way it was meant," Tru said. "As the truth."

She looked up into his eyes. The pain he had seen in her gaze had disappeared and in its place, a grudging appreciation. "Sometimes you can be a real nice guy, Harry Truman Hallihan," she said with a smile.

"And other times?" he prompted, oddly pleased at her improving opinion of him.

"Let's not get started on that now," she said wryly. "I've got work to do." Caroline turned and headed for the bedrooms. She was just about to knock on the master bedroom door when Tru grabbed her by the arm and stopped her. "What do you think you're doing?" he whispered.

"I'm going to help Ellis and Marianne work this disagreement out. It's important to face their problems, not run from them. They need to learn the proper way to communicate."

Tru dragged Caroline back down the hall into her bedroom and silently closed the door behind them. "Caroline, I don't think either one of them is interested in communicating right now. Maybe it would be best to leave them alone."

Caroline walked over to the wall and pressed her ear against it. "I don't hear anything."

"What do you expect to hear? They're in separate rooms."

"I *know* I can help them," she declared. "I have to help them. I should talk to Ellis first. He seems more amenable to counseling."

"Why are you so determined to fix their marriage? Like you said, you can't force people to love each other. If they're not happy, they should just divorce and get it over with."

She shook her head. "In this particular case, I have to try." She paused for a moment, as if deciding whether to continue. "I overheard Marianne talking in the ladies' room the night of the reception. It seems her money finances Ellis's company. If they get divorced, Ellis will probably lose the company and I'll lose my chance for a television talk show. If there is any chance to keep them together, I have to do it."

A surge of guilt washed over him. He was looking for a neat and tidy end to the Stones's marriage and Caroline was desperate to patch it up. He felt like a first-class heel, a slimeball, a sleaze, and every other disparaging name she'd called him in their short history together. "Are you doing this for them or for you?"

She pulled her ear away from the wall and turned back to him. "Does it really matter?" she asked.

"What if they don't want your help? Maybe they're beyond help."

"No marriage is beyond help. Except for mine," she added distractedly. "I know if I could get them both into counseling, I could make them see that."

"Maybe there's nothing left to save."

She crossed her arms in front of her and stared at him warily. "Why are you so dead set against me trying?"

"I'm not. I—I hope you succeed," he lied.

"I will, as long as you don't plan to participate in anymore extramarital activities with Ellis's wife. What did you think you were doing with Marianne?"

He shrugged. "Like I told Ellis, I thought she was you."

"You thought she was me and you kissed her like that?"

"Yeah, that's about it." He paused and watched her questioningly, a smile quirking his lips.

"What are you grinning at?" she asked, annoyed. "You're not lying to me, are you?"

"No," Tru replied. "I'm just surprised that you believe me."

"Of course, I believe you," Caroline said. "Why wouldn't I? I've known Marianne was after you since the night of the reception. Another little tidbit I overheard in the bathroom."

"And you didn't tell me?"

"Your ego is already overinflated. I didn't need to add more hot air. Besides, you do have a habit of kissing me whenever the whim strikes you. If you say you're telling the truth, then I believe you."

"For a marriage counselor, you don't know much about marriage, do you?"

She frowned. "What is that supposed to mean?"

"Here's a hypothetical situation for you, Dr. Leighton. Let's just say you *are* my wife. First, I accuse you of having an affair with another man. Then, you catch me in the arms of another woman. And now you forgive me, without a second thought. What's wrong with this picture, Doc?"

"What would you have me do? Punch her in the nose? Attempt murder? I tried to kick you out earlier, but you refused to leave, so that idea was out."

"Get mad, Caroline. Show your husband that you give a damn."

"Anger is counterproductive in this situation. Trust and honest communication are the most important tools in solving problems like these."

"Come on," he chided. "Drop the marriage counselor talk. You don't *really* trust me, do you?"

She looked at him long and hard. "No, I don't. Not entirely, if I'm to be candid."

"So, you just caught your husband kissing another woman. You don't trust him. Tell him how you really feel."

She rolled her eyes and gave him a long-suffering look. "You're not my husband," she replied calmly. "And it doesn't matter how I feel."

"But what if I *was* your husband?" Tru goaded. "Wouldn't you at least be a little angry? Be truthful, Caroline. You're steamed. I can tell. I can see those little heat waves coming off the top of your head. See there, you're turning red. You better let it blow before you explode."

"All right, maybe I was a bit perturbed," she conceded. "But not nearly enough to turn red and explode."

Tru chuckled and shook his head. "A bit perturbed," he mimicked. "How very civilized. This isn't a damn tea party, Caroline, this is a marriage. Show me how you really feel, not how you want me to *think* you feel. Fight for me."

"Just what are you getting at, Tru?"

"You maintain this oh-so-proper facade. The dispassionate professional with all the right answers, everything arranged and itemized on all those neat little lists of yours. But that's not who you are. You tried to be that woman for Edward, and look at what happened. You bottled everything up inside of you and stuffed a big cork in it. I know there's a passionate woman inside you somewhere, Caroline. She comes out every evening on your radio show."

"What do you want from me?" she demanded.

"I want you to tell me how you really feel."

"All right!" she snapped. "I'm angry. Are you satisfied now? I walk into the room and you're rolling around on the couch in a lip-lock with Marianne Stone. You're supposed to be my husband and she's the wife of a business associate. Of course, I'm angry."

Tru gasped in mock surprise. "You're angry? But you have nothing to be angry about."

She looked at him in utter confusion, the wind suddenly taken out of her sails. "Well . . . there . . . that's exactly what I told you before," she stammered. "I have nothing to be angry about. Confrontation is not going to—"

"Marianne kisses much better than you do," Tru commented blandly. "She's much more . . . enthusiastic."

He watched her spine stiffen and her green eyes flash fire. "If you think you can goad—"

"And she's got a terrific body. Don't you think she has a terrific body? Not that your body is bad, but . . . wow, she has a terrific body."

"You are disgusting," Caroline ground out. "Is that all that matters to you, a great body? You're about as shallow as a mud puddle, Tru Hallihan. There's a lot more to a woman than her body. What about her mind? Doesn't that matter to you at all? Sure, she might be enjoyable in bed, but you can't spend your whole life in bed. Sooner or later you have to get up and sit across from her at the breakfast table and communicate. Then what are you going to talk about? Her breasts? Well, that would make interesting early morning conversation—for about a minute. Then what?"

Tru smiled. This was *his* Caroline—fire and passion—not the woman she tried so hard to be. Not the woman that married Edward or the woman with a penchant for lists. This was the woman he wanted in his arms, in his bed, and in his life. "Well, I guess—"

"And just how do you know she kisses better than me?" she continued, ignoring his interjection. "You've never really kissed me. Unless you can call that sorry little peck on the cheek down on the pier a kiss. That wasn't a real kiss. And those other kisses, they were nothing. You have no idea how I kiss. You wouldn't know how to handle how I kiss, buster."

"Try me," Tru said.

Her eyes narrowed in rage, she placed her palms on his cheeks and pulled him toward her, standing on her tiptoes until they looked directly at each other. When he covered his mouth with hers, he expected the kiss to be hard with anger, but it wasn't. Her lips were soft and her mouth was pliant. She wrapped her arms around his neck and deepened the kiss, tentatively touching her tongue to his. A rush of desire shot through him and he pulled her closer, her breasts crushed against his chest. A deep moan rumbled in his throat.

Slowly, he felt her relinquish control and the kiss was no longer a challenge, but a shared experience. She drew back and nibbled at his lower lip, then traced a teasing line of tiny kisses along his jaw, her breath quickening with each inch. She was right. He had no idea how she kissed.

He cupped her chin in his palm and gently directed her back to his mouth and she opened to him again, this time with more confidence, more longing. She tasted so sweet and so warm, like a fine wine that was meant to be savored for an entire evening.

His hands drifted to her waist and he pulled her hips closer, fitting her against his thighs and pressing his hardness against her belly. She shifted against him, the contact sending a frisson of raw hunger ripping though him. He felt as if he were ready to explode. He stepped back and drew a deep, fortifying breath. Her eyes fluttered open and she looked up at him. Every shred of resistance she'd ever offered him was now gone and all he could see in her dazed expression was astonishment. The kiss had rocked her as deeply as it had him.

She swallowed convulsively. "I—I—don't know what to—"

He placed his finger over her lips and smiled. "The first word that comes into your mind," he murmured. "Don't think, just feel." His mouth touched her neck just below her ear and she sighed.

"Yes," she murmured.

He slid his hands to her waist and grabbed the belt to her robe, then waited.

"Open," she said.

He tugged at the knot and parted the silk, then pushed the robe over her shoulders and let it slide down her arms to the floor. She wore a white cotton nightgown beneath, the fabric so sheer she might as well have worn nothing. He placed his palms on her shoulders and toyed with the lace-edged straps, kneading her shoulders with his fingertips. Forget every opinion he'd ever had about her individual features. Put together, Caroline Leighton had an incredibly alluring body, one he wanted to explore, inch by beautiful inch.

Closing her eyes, she tipped her head back and bit her lower lip with perfect, white teeth. She drew a deep breath and shuddered. "Lower," she murmured.

His pulse raced but his hands moved with excruciating calm. He stopped and waited, his palms just below her collarbone.

"Lower," she moaned, her voice breathy and deep. He could listen to that voice all night, like raw silk sliding over his senses, whispering words of passion, urging him on.

He cupped her breasts in his palms and she sucked in a quick breath and held it for a long time, until his thumbs brushed across her hardened nipples. Then, she let it out slowly, reluctantly, her eyes still tightly closed, as if with the breath she released her anxiety, her restraint. A smile touched the corners of her mouth and he felt his insides go weak with desire. He wanted to see that smile, to hear her cries, and to watch her expression dissolve into pure, unrestrained pleasure.

She stood as still as a statue, a warm, living, breathing statue. He fought the urge to drag her over to the bed and stretch his body over hers. He was afraid that if he tried to move she might awaken from her sensual trance and her reticence would return. Bending down, he touched his mouth to the white cotton over her nipple, wetting it with his lips and tongue until he tasted her skin beneath.

"Oh," she breathed. "Oh, my." She burrowed her fingers into his hair and pressed him closer. He nibbled gently and listened as her breathing accelerated. If he could have made love to her standing in the middle of the room, he surely would have. But she was leaning heavily against him, as if her knees had gone weak. And he was in no condition to hold them both up.

"Caroline," he whispered, his mouth pressed against the soft mound of her breast.

"Umm," she replied.

His mouth drifted back up to hers. "Sweetheart," he murmured, his lips caressing hers.

"Sweetheart," she repeated softly.

He suddenly felt nervous, unsure, as if his next word or action might destroy the uncurbed lust that lingered over them both. He had always been so confident with women, but with Caroline, it was different. What she felt, what she thought, mattered to him. She wasn't a casual fling, a one-night stand. She was more, so much more.

"I want to make love to you," he whispered, his mouth against her ear. He pulled back then, at the same time both dreading and anticipating her response.

Her eyes opened lazily and she looked up at him. Relief washed over him as he saw only passion and desire in their green depths.

"Tell me you want me as much as I want you," he said.

"I want you," she stated, as if there were no other answer to be considered.

He cupped her face in his hands and kissed her long and deep. Her fingers clutched his wrists as if she were ready to sink to the floor. In one smooth motion, he scooped her up into his arms and carried her over to the bed, their mouths still melded in an urgent kiss.

Gently, he laid her across the bed, then sank down over top of her. He braced his arms on either side of her body, their only contact from the waist down. She opened her eyes and stared up at him, then smiled. Reaching up, she traced his bottom lip with her finger.

"Tru," she said, her voice ragged with desire. "I want you to promise me something."

He pressed his hips against hers, his erection hard and unyielding against her body, blatant proof of the passion yet to come. "I can't promise you anything, Caroline. Except that I know it's going to be good between us."

"That's not what I'm looking for," she said. "I—I want you to understand that this is purely a physical thing. And when it's over, that's all that it will ever be."

Tru stared at her, trying to read her expression. He saw only guilelessness in her liquid eyes. That and a tiny glimmer of apprehension. He couldn't believe what she was saying. She was letting him off the hook, offering him sex without expectations, satisfaction without guilt. But even though he would have jumped at the chance in the past, this particular offer seemed downright disagreeable.

It suddenly struck him that he didn't want casual sex. He wanted to make love to Caroline, not just in a physical way, but in a deeper, more enduring way. And he wanted to know that tonight wouldn't be the only time. He'd give up the case, the money, everything to ensure that they'd have a shot at another night together.

"I'm not sure I understand what you're saying," he murmured.

"I want what happens here tonight to stay in this bedroom. It begins and ends here. I know that you can't make a commitment and that you have no interest in a deeper relationship. And I want you to know that it doesn't matter. I don't want anything more."

"Why not?" he asked, anxious to hear her explanation.

"Because I know you're not capable of loving me. And I'm not going to try to make you feel something you don't feel. We've both known from the beginning that we weren't made for each other. But there's always been this attraction between us. If we have sex, maybe our curiosity will be appeased and we can both go on with our lives as if we never met."

"This is what you want?" Tru asked, anger raking through his soul. How could he have been so stupid, to think that there might be something more between them than just simple lust.

"It seems to be the most sensible course of action," she replied. "Wouldn't you agree?"

He forced a smile and controlled his temper. "Sure. I understand."

She smiled in return, satisfied with their agreement. Then she reached up and wove her fingers through his hair. Slowly, she pulled him toward her and kissed him. His arms buckled and he moaned as his body covered hers completely. An overwhelming need to possess her pulsed through his veins, liquid and warm, driven by his heart, not his mind.

His anger dissolved at her touch and he gave himself over to pure instinct, deepening their kiss, molding her body to his. But somewhere in the hidden corners of his mind, beyond instinct and beyond lust, a tiny voice told him to stop. Making love to her would not drive them apart as Caroline had hoped. It would only serve to intensify their attraction, for he knew, as soon as he buried himself inside her, there would be no turning back.

He rolled off of her and sat up on the edge of the bed. Bracing his elbows on his knees, he raked his hands through his hair and sighed. "I can't do this," he muttered, hardly able to believe his own words.

She sat up beside him and touched his shoulder hesitantly. "Did I do something wrong?" she asked.

"No," he said. He paused for a moment. "Maybe," he amended.

"I know I'm not very good at this," she said dejectedly. "And I know it's been a long time. But I thought it would be like riding a bike. I thought I'd at least be able to get past the preliminaries before veering into the ditch. Was I that bad? Please, be honest."

"It wasn't your... performance," he said. "It's me. It's my problem. I just can't go through with this."

"You mean you can't... you can't..." She cleared her throat. "Perform?"

He turned around, nettled by her assumption. "No! That's not it," he explained. "It's just that I don't want to... perform." He shook his head and pressed the heels of his hands into his eyes. "Geez, I never thought I'd hear those words coming out of my mouth. I must be going nuts."

A pained expression flitted across her flushed features and then it was gone, hidden behind a composed facade. "I understand. I don't... turn you on."

"Caroline, you have no idea what you do to me," he said. He stood up next to the bed and looked down at her, sorely tempted to ignore his conscience and give in to his desire. She looked so young and sweet in her prissy white nightgown. But he knew what kind of woman he'd find when he pulled the nightgown off. And that woman was hell to resist.

"Not a clue," he muttered. "I think it would be best if I found somewhere else to sleep. I'll see you in the morning."

He thought walking to the door was the hardest thing he'd ever done. And after he closed it behind him he was certain *that* act was even more difficult. But as he flopped down on the couch in the living room, his body still aroused, he knew the worst was yet to come. He'd spend the rest of the night, wide awake, and thinking of her alone, warm, aroused, and just down the hall.

And he'd spend the rest of his life wondering how good it could have been between them.

"I KNEW IT WOULD HAPPEN if I waited too long," Caroline cried, burying her face in her hands. "I've completely lost my ability to attract a man sexually. Not that I ever was any good at it."

Aurora lay on Caroline's office couch, lazily flipping through a deck of tarot cards. "I just asked how your weekend at Lake Arrowhead went," Aurora said, clearly baffled by Caroline's outburst. "What does fresh air and solitude have to do with your sex life?"

Caroline looked up across her desk and gave her friend a woeful smile. Then she covered her face with her hands again. "My quiet weekend turned into the worst battle since Normandy," she said. "All that was missing was the heavy artillery."

"Would you like to explain?"

Caroline calmly folded her hands in front of her. "Ellis showed up at the lake house. After that, Tru showed up with the silly notion that I was there to meet Ellis for an illicit rendezvous. Then Marianne Stone showed up and Ellis and I caught her kissing Tru. Then there was this big fight and Marianne and Ellis both stormed off to separate bedrooms. Then, somehow, I'm not sure how it happened, Tru and I ended up in the same bedroom. He tried to seduce me, then I tried to seduce him. Anyway, he ended up sleeping on the couch and I ended up sleeping alone. I woke up yesterday morning and everyone was gone. At first I thought it was all a bad dream, but now I'm pretty sure that it happened."

"You tried to seduce Tru Hallihan?" Aurora asked with a giggle. "I knew there was a reason I decided to come into the office on a Sunday. I had this funny premonition when I woke up this morning. Tell Aurora every little detail. From the beginning."

"That about sums it up," Caroline said. "I've been sitting here trying to list all the reasons why it went wrong, but I just can't figure it out." She handed Aurora her list. "Tru has made it clear from the very start that he is not looking for a relationship. And I'm sensible enough to know that he's not the man of my dreams. So I tried to make things easy for him. I assured him that I wouldn't be looking for anything beyond a physical encounter. That's when he got out of bed and walked out of the room."

Just the memory of it brought a hot flush of embarrassment to Caroline's face. She'd lain awake for nearly the entire night, tempted to go to him, to fix whatever mistake she had made. Finally, after hours of tossing and turning, she'd drifted off. And when she'd awoke the next morning, the house was empty.

"Go ahead," Caroline said. "Tell me what I did wrong."

Aurora studied her for a long moment. "He's in love with you," she stated.

"What?" Caroline gasped.

"He's in love with you. He may not know it yet, but he is."

"That's ridiculous. If he was in love with me, why did he run out of the bedroom like his hair was on fire?"

"Because he's in love with you. And you bruised his ego."

Caroline stared at Aurora, dumbfounded and utterly speechless. It couldn't possibly be true. The man had made it clear from the very start that he didn't believe in a forever kind of love.

"I'm not saying that he *knows* he loves you," Aurora added. "If he's like most men, he'll deny it for a while, he may even try to forget you with another woman. But sooner or later it's going to hit him like a truck and he's going to realize that he can't live without you. And then you better watch out. The way you describe Tru Halli-han, he's not the type to quit until he gets what he wants."

"But he is entirely wrong for me," Caroline said fran-tically. She opened her desk drawer and pulled out a file folder. "Here, I made a list. These are all the reasons why we can never have a relationship. See." She held up the paper and pointed to it. "Twenty-three major reasons. And there are more, but I didn't think it was necessary to list the minor points."

Aurora snatched the paper from Caroline's fingers and gave it a quick perusal. Then she crumpled it in one hand

and tossed it over her shoulder. "Give me a piece of paper," Aurora demanded. "And a pencil. I'm going to make you a list of all the reasons you're right for each other."

Caroline did as her friend asked, then watched her scribble something on the yellow legal pad. It took Aurora only a few seconds before she looked up and smiled.

"There you go," Caroline said in disgust. "That certainly didn't take long. Five seconds and you've listed all the reasons why I could have a future with Tru Hallihan. Not very encouraging is it?"

Aurora turned the pad around and held it up for Caroline to read. Written in huge block letters was one simple word. "Destiny?" Caroline asked.

"Cosmic forces beyond your control. Fate. Karma. Kismet. Call it what you like, Caro. But understand one thing. You can't fight it. You were meant to be with Tru Hallihan. The energy is so strong between you two, even I can feel it."

"But he's all wrong for me. Just look at my 'Six Steps to Marital Success.' First there's compatibility. We don't share any interests in common, and whenever we're together we end up fighting. Then there's compromise; Tru Hallihan is as stubborn as a mule, and I don't think he'd ever change. We don't communicate, half the time I can't figure out what he's thinking. It's like he's from a different planet. And lately, I get the distinct impression that he's hiding something from me. He *does* care for me, at least a little bit. But as far as commitment goes, he has no interest in a happily ever after. One out of six. The marriage would be doomed."

"Caroline, forget your lists. How does the man make you feel?"

"Nervous and a little sick to my stomach," she replied.

"What else?"

"Warm and fluttery and breathless. When he touches me, I can't think of anything but the places where his hand and my skin meet. And when he kisses me, I want it to go on and on."

"Caroline, you've spent your entire professional career trying to analyze the vagaries of love. Maybe it's time you stopped using your head and started paying attention to your heart."

"I can't do that. That goes against everything I tell my radio listeners and my patients. It's important to approach relationships in a logical, thoughtful manner."

"Love happens in different ways to different people, Caro. Maybe you're not meant to love with your head."

"Maybe I'm not meant to love at all," she murmured.

Aurora popped off the couch and handed Caroline the notepad. "I don't believe that. If I were you, I'd give Mr. Hallihan another chance. He might just turn out to be the man of your dreams."

"Not a chance," Caroline grumbled.

"And I want you to do one more thing, Caro," Aurora said with a smile.

"What's that?"

"I want you to make another list—a list of all the reasons you're going to stop making lists. And after you're done with that, I think you better sit down and have a little heart-to-heart with your heart."

Caroline watched Aurora stroll out of her office. She grabbed the pad and ripped off the top sheet, ready to crumple it in her hand. But instead, she placed it in front of her and stared at the word.

Destiny. Somehow, it was hard to believe that out of all the men in the world, she was destined to fall in love with Tru Hallihan. But then, what did she know about cosmic forces?

# 7

THE TRAFFIC was surprisingly light for the noon hour as Caroline turned right on Lasky Drive. She spotted a place to park on the street just a block from the restaurant and decided to avoid the parking lot and grab the exercise while she could. The balmy autumn breeze and a brisk walk would help to clear the chaos in her mind.

Since she had returned from Lake Arrowhead, she had tried to purge herself of all thoughts of Tru Hallihan and focus on her work. She had overbooked her appointments in hopes that she'd be able to lose herself in someone else's problems rather than her own. And when she wasn't seeing clients, she threw herself into research and preparation for her first show. She'd even been to her health club three times that week.

But no matter how hard she tried to control her thoughts, they constantly returned to Aurora's strange proclamation and Tru's even stranger behavior. Could the man really be in love with her and not know it? He seemed like the type of guy who would certainly know his own mind, at least when it came to women. And he had made it blatantly clear to her that he had no interest in marriage or even a serious entanglement. Tru's views on romantic commitment were like a quake-proof building. He might roll a tiny bit with whatever seismic event came his way, but he wasn't about to tumble, no matter how the earth shook.

And that's all she'd been to him, just a brief blip on the Richter scale of romance. She couldn't even entice him into making love to her, even with her assurances that it would only be a physical encounter. If she'd told him she expected anything more, he probably would have bolted before the first button had been undone. As it was, they hadn't made it much further than the bed before he backed out.

If Tru Hallihan really loved her, as Aurora suspected, he would have made love to her that night. She flashed back to the scene in the bedroom, to Tru's head bent over her breast, to the feel of his hair between her fingers and the touch of his warm, wet tongue as it caressed her nipple. She caught her breath as a wave of desire washed through her body and pooled at her core.

Groaning inwardly, Caroline snatched her purse from the seat beside her and stepped out of her car. She would drive herself crazy trying to figure out what went wrong that night. Tru Hallihan was out of her life. Their "marriage" was over. And it was time to move on. After all, there were other fish in the ocean. Nice, gentle, loyal fish with no aversion to marriage. She'd do well to catch one of those, for if she continued to be attracted to sharks, she'd end up being eaten alive.

Caroline tucked her purse under her arm and walked purposefully down the sidewalk. She had a lunch meeting scheduled with Ellis at Johnny's, an elegant Beverly Hills restaurant and a favorite spot for the Hollywood set. Though the expected agenda included talk of her show, she intended to use the opportunity to bring up Ellis's marital problems. If she could convince the Stones to try counseling, there was a good chance that her show would have a future beyond the next few weeks.

As Caroline approached the restaurant, she glanced up and down the street, checking for Ellis's car. She saw the black Benz parked across from the entrance. Her gaze drifted to a car parked three spaces behind the Benz and a man who watched her from inside the nondescript sedan. She automatically glanced away, then realized that the man behind the dark glasses looked a lot like . . . Tru Hallihan.

She snapped her gaze back to the car, but the man was gone. The sedan appeared empty, the window revealing only a reflection of the noontime sun. "You're losing your mind, Caroline," she murmured to herself, shaking her head.

The inside of the restaurant was comfortable, yet posh, with fine china, silver and crystal on each of the linen-covered tables. Johnny's was one of Caroline's favorite restaurants, partly because of the lovely decor but mostly because of the smoked quail salad. The maître d' escorted her to a table along the windows which overlooked a lovely terrace garden with a fountain and brightly colored flowers.

Ellis stood as the maître d' seated her. "Caroline, it's good to see you again."

She smiled and shook his hand. "Ellis, it's nice to see you, too." The pleasantries couldn't cover Ellis's obvious tension and discomfort. Last Saturday's debacle at the lake house seemed to hang over the table like a dark cloud. Caroline decided that it would be best to broach the subject immediately and clear the air. But Ellis beat her to the punch.

"Caroline, I want to apologize for my wife's behavior the other night. Marianne is a very. . .emotional woman and she sometimes has a tendency to leap before she looks. She somehow got the notion in her head that you and I are involved outside of our business dealings. Her behavior with Lance was simply her way of striking back at me."

Caroline reached over and placed her hand on his sympathetically. "I'm glad you brought this up, Ellis."

"I'm sorry if she caused you and Lance any trouble," he continued. "I heard him leave in the middle of the night. When Marianne took off an hour later, I decided to follow her and settle this thing between us."

"And did you settle it?" Caroline asked.

"No, not any more than we've settled anything lately. We seem to be at a standoff. Marianne is certain I'm cheating on her and nothing I can say can convince her otherwise. I think her father has been inciting her. He never liked me. He thought Marianne was marrying beneath herself when she married me. And he can't stand the fact that I've used her money to start my own production company."

"*Are* you cheating on her, Ellis?"

He glanced away, staring out at the garden, then shook his head. "I came close, once. But no, technically, I haven't cheated on my wife. But that really doesn't make a difference. Marianne thinks I did. She knows me better than anyone on this earth and she sensed something was wrong. I've wanted to tell her the truth for a long time, but I'm afraid I'm going to lose her."

"Because of the money?"

Ellis laughed. "No," he said. "The money doesn't mean a thing to me. It was never about the money." His gaze returned to the garden. "Marianne and I met at a big premiere party. I was working as a publicity assistant on the movie and I think she decided to go out with me just to make her father squirm. It was love at first sight. Destiny. And I married Marianne because I loved her, no matter what her father might have told her. I still do love her. I'd give up everything—my company, the house in Bel Air, everything—if we could have that back."

"Have you told her this, Ellis?"

He shook his head and looked back at her. "No. Even if I could get her to sit down and talk to me, I don't think she'd listen. Her father's got her convinced that I'm a bum. And maybe I am. After all, I'm just a house painter's son from Reseda." He shook his head. "How do you and Lance do it? You two are crazy about each other, anyone can see that."

Caroline shifted uneasily in her chair and toyed with her fork. "Well, we've worked hard at our marriage," Caroline lied. "It's not always easy, believe me." It was darn near impossible, to tell the truth. She and Tru had just as many problems as Ellis and his wife, and they weren't even married!

"You know," Ellis continued, "Lance and I have a lot in common. We grew up in the same neighborhood. He's struggling to build a career in this town, like me, and his wife pays the mortgage. How do you keep that from poisoning your marriage?"

"I—I guess we just try to focus on our feelings for each other," Caroline replied, remembering Aurora's method for marriage. "On what's important. The rest just doesn't matter."

"That's how it used to be with me and Marianne."

"Well, maybe, with a little hard work, we can get that back for you two. I'd like to suggest counseling for you and Marianne. I'd be happy to help, but if you'd feel more comfortable with someone else, I could recommend a colleague. But either way, I want you to sit down and tell your wife everything you've told me."

"I don't think Marianne would agree to counseling."

"Then come by yourself, but let her know where you're going. Sooner or later Marianne will realize that you want to work on your marriage and maybe she'll decide to come along."

Ellis smiled and squeezed her hand. "I wish I was as confident as you."

"It sounds trite, and my fellow marriage counselors would probably kill me for saying this, but just remember that love really can conquer all—with a little hard work."

The rest of the lunch passed with a discussion of Caroline's first show over a perfect smoked quail salad with balsamic dressing, and a sinful chocolate soufflé for dessert. As she and Ellis walked outside, she realized that she hadn't thought of Tru Hallihan for nearly an hour. She consciously avoided looking across the street for the dark sedan and instead looked up at Ellis.

"Talk to Marianne," she said. "Then give me a call and we'll set up an appointment."

Ellis grabbed her hand, then bent to kiss her cheek. "Thanks, Caroline. We've got a production meeting scheduled for your pilot early next week and I'll go over your ideas with the producers. We should be ready to tape the test show sometime next month. I'll fax you the schedule as soon as it's set. And I promise to try talking to Marianne."

Caroline smiled then turned to walk to her car. She was halfway down the block when Ellis's car passed by. He beeped his horn and she waved. But her hand froze in midwave as the dark sedan drove by an instant later. She glimpsed at the driver, and though she could barely see his profile through the glare on the window, a overwhelming sense of familiarity shot though her.

"You *are* losing your mind, Caroline," she murmured. "Next thing you know, you'll see Tru Hallihan driving a city bus . . . you'll see him in your morning coffee . . . he'll appear out of thin air. You have got to get a hold of yourself, before the man drives you crazy!"

*"GOOD EVENING, Los Angeles. This is KTRL, Talk Radio L.A. and you're listening to 'Making Your Marriage Work.' I'm your host, Dr. Carly Lovelace and tonight we're discussing commitment. Let's take another call. This is Dr. Lovelace and you're on the air."*

*"Dr. Lovelace, my boyfriend says he loves me, but he just won't commit to a permanent relationship. I want to get married, but how can I make my marriage work, when I can't even get to the altar?"*

*"A recent survey found that four out of five single women say the single men they know want to avoid commitment. On the other hand, studies show that unmarried men die earlier than married men. So, does this mean that men commit because they want to live longer, or does it mean living a single life-style is hazardous to a man's health? I don't know what it means, but I do know there are some specific reasons why men avoid commitment.*

*"Number one—the grass is always greener syndrome. Men are afraid that if they commit, they might regret their choice later on. They're afraid someone a little greener and a little fresher might come along."*

Tru adjusted the volume on the car radio until he could hear every subtle nuance of her voice. The grass was always greener. Somehow, he had a hard time believing that he'd ever find someone more fascinating, more beautiful, more exasperating, than Caroline Leighton.

He might spend the rest of his life looking, but he'd always compare every woman he met to her.

*"Men are also concerned about the financial responsibility that comes along with marriage. Will my wife continue working or will I be completely responsible for our financial future? What about a house? Retirement? This is a tremendous pressure."*

"Hey, no pressure there," Tru muttered. Caroline would never want to give up her career, especially if she got the television job. And he would barely be able to support her on what he made as a P.I. Maybe with the security retainer from Simon Marshall, he'd have more to offer. But there was the rub. If he proved grounds on Ellis and she found out, she'd never forgive him. And if he didn't, a solid financial future was still a few years off.

"So, I'm one for two," he murmured. "But, Caroline said money didn't matter. All right, maybe I'm one and a half for two."

*"Another reason men don't feel pressured to commit these days is that they can have all the benefits of marriage without getting married. The 'Why Buy The Cow Theory.' Regular sex without marriage, a hired housekeeper to clean up after them, nutritious homecooked meals, and no responsibilities. Though it doesn't all come free, at least they won't have to fear waking up to the same woman day after day. Fear of boredom is another factor that keeps men from committing."*

Tru considered the possibility. What would it be like to wake up to Caroline's face every morning? To fall asleep with her wrapped in his arms every night? The thought wasn't distasteful in the least. He couldn't imagine being bored with her. And the benefits of seeing her whenever he wanted were pretty tempting.

So, he wasn't reluctant to commit for the reasons she outlined. But there must be other reasons why the prospect of a serious relationship didn't appeal to him. He waited for those reasons to come to him and when they didn't, he channeled his mind and tried to think of at least one reason to avoid Caroline Leighton. He flipped off the radio, unable to concentrate with her voice all around him.

"Come on, Hallihan," he prodded. "You can at least find one reason not to have a serious relationship with Caroline." He considered the problem for a good fifteen minutes before he gave up. The only thing he could come up with was Marshall's twenty-thousand dollars for catching Ellis in the act. But that didn't really count because that had nothing at all to do with his feelings for Caroline.

Suddenly, the case didn't make a whole lot of difference. It had consumed his life for the week before he had found her in his telephoto lens. And every day since then, it had become less and less important. Hell, he could get where he wanted to be without the twenty thousand dollars. He nearly had enough in investments now to afford a plush office and a secretary and, thereby, make the move on a few corporate security accounts.

Tru started the car and popped it into gear. As of this moment, Tru Hallihan was off the Stone case. In two weeks of investigation, he had found no proof that Ellis Stone was having an extramarital affair. The address book had been a bust. Surveillance uncovered zilch. Every lead he'd gotten had been explained away as a business contact.

As for Caroline, he'd have to trust his instincts. She wasn't having an affair with Ellis Stone. Even the thought of it seemed ludicrous now. He had asked and she had told him the truth. He believed her. Besides, they were way too public with their meetings and she was way to principled for an affair with a married man. She couldn't have fallen into bed with Tru as she had, with her lover in the other room.

Glancing over his shoulder, he pulled a U-turn in front of the restaurant, leaving Ellis and his business associate to their dinner. Thirty minutes later, he parked in front of KTRL's Burbank studio. The main door was locked as was the employee entrance, but a service door next to the loading dock was open. He watched a custodian toss two bags of trash into a bin, then plod back inside. A few seconds later, Tru sneaked through the unlocked door.

He came to a dead stop once inside the huge boiler room. Her voice was everywhere, echoing off the concrete block walls and the steel girders, this time richer and more vibrant than on his car radio. He felt as if she were in the room with him, then realized that it was only the station's P.A. system. The sound of slow footsteps punctuated her words and Tru silently slipped behind a row of battered tool cabinets as the janitor returned.

*"Dr. Lovelace, my problem has to do with sexual spontaneity. There are times that my husband decides he wants to make love and he wants to do it now—on the kitchen table, in the garage, wherever he happens to be at the moment. I prefer to set the mood. I like to fix my hair and makeup, put on a sexy negligee, turn on some soft music and light some candles. He says this turns him off, not on. I don't understand."*

*"Spontaneous sex can be a wonderful way of expressing your love. We've often talked about performance anxiety in men and this is a perfect example. You've set the stage, all the props are in place, the costumes and makeup are perfect. Now all your husband has to do is*

*turn in an award-winning performance and the evening will be a resounding success. Men sometimes feel controlled by this type of atmosphere. And it can also make them think that you don't like sex, that all these accessories are simply a way of making sex more palatable for you. On the other hand, spontaneous sex can make you feel out of control and it lacks the romantic foreplay that women crave."*

"So, what should I do?"

*"Take one of my 'Six Steps to Marital Success' and put it to work. Compromise. I'm not saying you should relegate your sex life to the kitchen table, but try to enjoy your husband's overwhelming sexual desire for you every now and then, and indulge in a little spontaneous sex. Don't discard the romantic setup completely. Just don't force your husband to wait in bed, cooling his jets, while you make sure your mascara is perfect. Take care of those little details before he even walks in the bedroom door and I think he'll feel much less anxiety and you'll feel more in control."*

An image of Caroline, lying naked across his kitchen table, flashed through Tru's mind. His blood rushed from his limbs to his lap and he winced as he felt himself grow hard. He focused his concentration on the lazy whistle of the janitor and tried to regain control of his hormones. After a few deep breaths, he peeked around the edge of the cabinet.

The man sat on a stool, a huge rubber trash can in front of him. He slowly picked through the garbage, uncrumpling papers and reading them carefully as he listened to Caroline's show. Fortunately, employee espionage didn't hold his attention for long, and ten minutes later he wandered back through the door to the studios. Ten seconds after that, Tru followed him.

It wasn't hard to find Caroline. A long dimly lit hall-way led to three studios, each with an On Air sign above the door. Only one was illuminated. He quietly opened the door and stepped inside the nearly dark studio, expecting her to turn at the sound of his entrance. But her back was to him and her ears were covered with head-phones. The only light filtered through a small window which she faced, casting her features in a soft white glow. She spoke into a microphone suspended from the ceiling on a folding arm.

He pushed the door closed and listened as her voice weaved a spell around him in the silent vacuum of the studio. There were no sounds from outside, only the sound of her voice and his breathing. He waited, lean-ing back against the door, until she broke for a commer-cial and pulled off her headset.

"Two minutes, Carly." A woman's voice came through a small speaker near Caroline's hand. "Then I've got Edna from Oxnard on the line."

Caroline pushed a button on the control console and made a face into the window. "Again? Dana, the woman is seventy-three. Her husband is seventy-five. They should be happy they can still do it and stop complain-ing. What is it tonight?"

"Bondage. Edna's for it, her husband's not."

"Bondage," Caroline murmured to herself, shaking her head.

"Sounds like fun," Tru replied.

His softly spoken words were amplified by the dead air in the studio. She jumped in her chair and with a tiny shriek, spun around to face him. Squinting into the shadows, she searched for him. When her eyes found him, she opened her mouth as if to scream.

He stepped from the darkness near the door and drew a deep breath, then plunged in before she had a chance to make a sound. "All right," he said. "Here's the deal. I've been thinking about us, you and me. And I'd like to have a...relationship. A serious relationship. I know I'm not exactly the kind of guy you're used to, but—"

"What are you doing here?" she asked, finally finding her voice. "How did you get in?"

"Through the back door. Now, I know you probably have a list of all the qualities you're looking for in a guy, but I want you to know right now, I can't live up to one of your lists. You're— "

"One minute, Carly."

Tru looked in the direction of the console speaker. "Who is that?"

"My producer. She's right next door. Tru, I'm on the air. You have to leave."

"I'm not leaving, not until we get this straight between us."

"Carly, what's going on in there?"

Caroline turned back to the control panel and waved through the window, then pressed the intercom button. "It's nothing, Dana. I'm fine." She lifted her hand from the button and turned back to Tru. "Leave, now, before she sees you and calls security."

"Not until I take care of one thing."

Tru stepped across the room and grabbed the edges of her chair's seat. He pulled the chair toward him, out of the view of the window, and bent down on one knee. Furrowing his fingers through her hair, he gently drew her mouth down to his and covered it in a slow, tantalizing kiss.

"Thirty seconds," Dana warned.

He deepened the kiss, cradling her face in his hands and plunging his tongue into the soft recesses of her mouth. He felt her respond and the heat that he'd tried to ignore earlier came back, this time like a ball of fire, engulfing them both.

"AND YOU'RE ON in five, four..."

Tru pulled away and grabbed Caroline's headset, positioning it over her ears. With a firm shove and a satisfied grin, he sent her chair rolling across the floor toward the mike.

"...three, two, one. And you're on."

Caroline gulped and brushed her rumpled hair back from her face. "And we're ba—back," she stammered. "You're listening to... 'Making Your Marriage Work' and I'm Dr. Caro—Carly Lovelace. Our next call is from... from..." She glanced up at the window, frantically trying to remember what Dana had told her just a few minutes before. Edna, Dana mouthed. From Oxnard, Caroline remembered.

"And we have Edna from Oxnard on the line," she said, recovering smoothly. "Good evening, Edna. Tell us what's on your mind tonight."

Caroline pushed away from the microphone and stifled a sigh, listening distractedly through her headphones to Edna's septuagenarian sexual woes. She glanced furtively toward the door for Tru, then suddenly felt herself spun around in the opposite direction. He was still on his knees, hidden from Dana's sight. She shoved at his shoulder, then pointed at the door, but he didn't budge an inch. Instead, her grabbed her ankle and slipped off her shoe. Slowly, deliciously, he began to massage her foot.

She tried to pull away, but the touch of his fingers tenderly kneading her instep brought a soft moan to her throat. She felt detached from the scene before her, unable to hear anything but Edna's voice in her headphones, unable to protest without her words being broadcast all over Los Angeles, only able to feel his hands on her body. She closed her eyes and gave herself over to his silent ministrations, stretching her leg out in front of her and wiggling her toes. But when he placed her flexing foot against the solid ridge of his desire, her eyes snapped open.

He smiled and moved his fingers to her calf, sliding his palms enticingly from her ankle to her knee until she couldn't help but leave her foot exactly where he'd planted it. The heat from his hardness snaked its way from the sole of her foot, up her leg and into the growing warmth between her own legs. She pressed against him, then stroked her foot back and forth until he wrapped his fingers around her ankle to stop her.

Somewhere, in the back of her mind, she was aware of the voice coming through her headphones, but when Edna from Oxnard stopped speaking, it took several moments for her to realize that it was time for Dr. Lovelace to offer her advice.

Caroline reached overhead and yanked the microphone toward her. "I—I'd like you to tell me more, Edna," she said. "Tell me how you...feel." The last word was nearly a groan, as Tru's palms slipped under her skirt. He moved his fingers up along the outside of her thighs, then crossed over and brought his hands back down along the sensitive skin of her inner thighs, slowly, sensuously, until she thought she might scream. She shifted in her chair and parted her legs slightly, silently cursing the panty hose that kept his touch from making direct contract with her tingling skin.

Edna had stopped talking again. "Is there anything else you'd like to tell me, Edna?" she asked, her voice catching slightly. Usually, she couldn't wait to cut short Edna's long-winded dissertations on her quirky sex life, but tonight she felt a professional responsibility to listen to the whole story. The woman started in again and Caroline's attention immediately returned to Tru's hands.

He had worked his way up inside her tight skirt until his hands grasped her body just below her hips. As if he had read her mind, he snagged her panty hose in his fingers and pulled them down, working them beneath her and then off her legs. She was certain all L.A. could hear the sound of shredding nylon, but she didn't care. All she wanted was the heat of his strong, sure hands on her body.

Maybe it was good that she couldn't talk to him, couldn't stop him. She had no choice but to allow her reserve to melt beneath his touch. Edna was waiting again. She sucked in a long breath and turned back to the microphone.

"Edna, I—I think that your husband might be a—a bit set in his ways to try some of the more adventurous aspects of a bon-bondage." Caroline felt her skirt sliding up her thighs. "Discuss this matter with your husband. Unless he feels entirely—" her words caught in her throat for a instant and she coughed "—comfortable with this idea, I think it would be best to leave the handcuffs to the proper auth-authorities." His fingers brushed against her damp panties. She swallowed hard. "And now a word from our sponsors." The words came out in a rush.

She shoved the mike away and pushed off her headphones. Weaving her fingers through Tru's hair, she pulled his mouth against hers in a frantic, demanding kiss. She couldn't resist him anymore. Like a woman parched with thirst, she was nearly crazy for the taste of him on her lips, for the feel of him plundering her mouth with his tongue.

"Carly?" Dana's voice filtered through her foggy thoughts. "Carly, what's going on in there? We weren't scheduled for a commercial break until after the show, at the top of the hour. Traffic is going to have a fit if we don't follow the schedule."

Tru buried his face in the curve of her neck and she fumbled back for the intercom button. "Everything's fine, Dana," she called weakly. "Just a . . . frog in my . . . throat."

"Well, get the damn amphibian out of your throat. We're going to have to fill some air until the network feed comes in for the next show. Take one more call, but try to stretch it a little. You're on in five, four, three, two . . ."

Caroline grabbed her headphones from around her neck and snapped them over her ears. Tru let her go, his attention now diverted by the tiny buttons down the front of her silk blouse.

"We're back on the air," she said breathlessly. "Let's take another call."

One by one, he dispatched each button, then brushed the silk back. She pushed his hands away, determined to concentrate on her show. But he was not about to be deterred. His fingers traced the edges of her lace bra, dipping beneath the silky fabric until she was ready to rip the expensive piece of underwear off herself. He fumbled with the clasp at the front and the lacy lingerie slipped away from her breasts, baring them to his touch.

She heard the caller through her headset but could barely comprehend what the woman was saying. All her

thoughts were centered on the feel of Tru's mouth closing over her nipple, his tongue bringing the tip to a hard
peak.

"...my husband says that I should be more aggressive. He says that I should initiate sex every now and
then. I'm just not an aggressive person, Dr. Lovelace. I'd
be too embarrassed."

"It's important to understand the emotional risk involved in initiating sex," Caroline replied, fighting off the
waves of pleasure Tru's tongue brought forth. "Each time
your husband approaches you, he risks your rejection.
This makes him feel controlled and manipulated. Maybe
your husband would like you to share in that risk. Nothing turns a man on more ...than to know the woman he
loves ...wants him as much as he . . . wants her. And
now, I think it's time for another word from our sponsors."

Tru yanked her headphones off and tossed them to the
floor. His tongue found the hollow of her throat and he
began to scatter a path of kisses from there back to her
breast.

Dana's voice came over the intercom almost immediately. "You're lucky I'm such a great producer," she
said. "I just happened to find a Public Service An-
nouncement to play. What's wrong? Are you getting
laryngitis? I've got some tea and honey in here. Would
you like me to bring you some?"

Caroline fumbled for the intercom switch. "No!" she
cried. "No thanks. Just play a few more PSAs and then
sign off for me, would you, Dana? I want to ...rest
my...voice." Caroline gently pushed against Tru's
shoulders and stood. She closed the venetian blinds over
the window between the studios, then walked over to the
door and locked it. Without the light from the adjoining

studio, the soundproof room was bathed in shadows. Power lights from the tape machines and the control console glowed red and gold in the dark.

She watched as he stood, his gaze locked with hers. Slowly, she stripped off the jacket of her designer suit and let it drop to the floor. An incredible surge of feminine power washed over her as she watched his reaction. She tugged her blouse from the waistband of her skirt and let it hang open, barely revealing the curves of her breasts. His eyes drifted down and she moved until the silk parted a bit more.

In three short steps, he crossed the studio. His harsh breathing seemed amplified many times over in the still confines of the studio. He pushed her back against the soft soundproof foam that covered the walls and the door.

"Can she hear us?" he whispered against her ear.

Caroline shook her head and kissed his jaw. "Not unless I activate the intercom again."

He pulled back and smiled. "Good. Now, about this relationship of ours."

She pushed up on her toes and kissed him on the mouth. "I know," she said. "I think it's about to get serious."

"Very serious," he growled.

She had never felt such desire, such need in her life, not with Edward or any man who had come before. It both frightened and empowered her and she wanted to take the risk, to satisfy the craving that twisted through her body until she felt like a spring wound too tight. She would show him how she felt by actions, not by words. "I think it's time to even the score, don't you?" she asked.

He frowned.

"Take off your jacket," she said. "And your T-shirt."

"Doctor's orders?" he asked with a chuckle.

"Doctor's orders, Mr. Hallihan."

He grinned. "I love an aggressive woman."

She wriggled from his arms and snatched up her panty hose from the floor near the control console. She walked back to him and fluttered the nylons over his shoulders and down his chest. "And what about bondage?" she said, yanking the hose tight between her hands. "Or maybe spontaneous sex?"

He slipped out of his jacket, then tugged his shirt over his head. His chest was smooth and muscular with a fine tracing of hair that ran from the base of his neck to the top button of his jeans. She felt an urge to reach out and touch him, then realized that there was no longer any reason to bury her urges. Her palm skimmed his chest and came to rest over his heart. A rhythmic pulse, strong and solid, beat beneath her fingertips.

"Sweetheart, I'm open to anything you want to try." His pulse quickened beneath her hand. "But, if I were you, I wouldn't bother tying my hands. There's no way I'm going to keep from touching you when and where I want."

The panty hose drifted to the floor, forgotten. She wanted his hands on her body, tonight, tomorrow, forever. She pressed against him, her fingers splayed across his chest, her lips on the hard angle of his collarbone. He slipped his hands beneath her blouse and pulled it open until skin met skin, her breasts warm against his hard muscle and bone.

Slowly, she nuzzled his neck. "Make love to me, Tru. Now."

He pulled her over to the chair and sat down, trapping her against the control console. His movements were urgent, his control gone, his need evident in every tensed muscle. Gathering her skirt in his fists, he pushed it up until he reached her panties. Before she knew it, they were around her ankles. She kicked them away, then turned and grabbed her purse from the end of the console.

She opened it and withdrew a small foil packet. "I practice what I preach," she murmured, a flush creeping up her body.

"Umm, I can see that," he said, shuddering slightly as his fingers slipped between her legs. "I want to practice what you preach, too."

She was hot and wet and ready, so ready she could hear her own heartbeat in the silence of the studio. His touch was electric, sending jolts of anticipation straight to her core. Unable to resist, she began to move wantonly against his hand. She moaned as he brought her nearer to her peak, the sound filling the still air before it was absorbed by the walls.

She opened her eyes and drew a shaky breath, regaining a small thread of control. Then she reached over and pulled his belt open. He handled the buttons of his jeans, releasing himself to her touch. He was smooth and hard and as she quickly sheathed him, he sucked in his breath and bit back a groan.

He slouched down in the chair and rested his head against the back, then looked up at her. His heavy-lidded gaze wandered over her face. "I want to love you, Caroline," he murmured. "I want to try."

She brushed her finger across his mouth, a gentle sign of her assent. With that, he pulled her over him and pushed her skirt up. She lowered herself onto him until he probed at her moist entrance. She had never felt such overwhelming passion, such unquenchable hunger. She wanted to savor the feeling and at the same time she wanted to slake her need. He circled her waist and drew her down until he was buried to the hilt.

They moved together, as if they had made love many times before. And yet it seemed as if he were her first lover, so intense and alien were the sensations he induced from her body. Her release came fast and hard, shocking her with its ferocity. She trembled over him, unable to move, her body clenching and unclenching around him. And then, with a low groan, he joined her, shuddering beneath her and whispering her name in a mindless cadence.

When he had regained his breath Tru brushed his lips against her temple, "I know what I want," Tru murmured, "I want this to work. And I want you to help me make it work, Caroline. You don't have to decide now, but think about it."

Caroline didn't need time to decide. She loved him and it frightened her. But it was the only thing she really knew for sure.

# 8

CAROLINE PUSHED OPEN the door to the West Hollywood storefront. The lower floor housed a trendy antique clothing store and the upper floor, four offices. She scanned the list of occupants painted on the window as she walked through. Tru was listed third, right beneath Irving Mellman, Accountant, and Peeler's Party Strippers, and right above Sid Dempster, Hollywood Casting Agent. She climbed the narrow stairway to the second floor and knocked on the door labeled Hallihan Investigations.

She was taking a chance, hoping to find him here. She'd called and left a message with his answering service an hour ago, requesting that he meet her at his office at one o'clock sharp, but she had no idea if he had picked up his messages.

After a night of making love with Tru in her bed, she'd awakened that morning alone, the scent of his cologne on her pillows and a short note the only proof that he had been there. He'd leave the decision up to her, the note said. Either their relationship would be all or nothing. If the note wasn't enough, he had made his feelings clear over and over again during the course of their night together. He wanted her—and for more than just one night.

She had wanted to believe they could have a future. But with so many factors working against them already, the marriage counselor inside her could only toll the warning bells. If she was one of her patients, Dr. Caroline Leighton would recommend making a list of expectations, discussing that list with her potential partner, and deciding whether the man could make her happy. The list was tucked inside her purse and she was anxious to review it with Tru.

She had considered stopping by Tru's apartment, but suspected she'd be better off discussing the matter on more businesslike turf. Using a typical bachelor tactic, she had decided that *his* turf would be best. If things didn't fall into place, she could always exit his office gracefully, saving them both an uncomfortable parting.

"He's not in," a voice called from behind her.

Caroline spun around to find a half-naked woman standing in the doorway across the hall. Plastic fruit strategically covered the most erotic parts of her body but the other parts were left completely naked. She watched Caroline through heavily lined eyes, picking distractedly at the clump of grapes that covered her left breast.

"Do—do you know when he'll be back?" Caroline asked.

The woman shook her head, nearly dislodging the Carmen Miranda hat perched on her peroxide blond hair. "He don't check in with me, sweetie," she said in a high-pitched baby doll voice. "Though I wouldn't mind if he did. He's a real stud, that Truman is. You looking for a P.I.?"

"Not exactly," Caroline replied. "I'm just a friend of his."

"Well, if you was looking for a dick, Tru's the best."

Caroline swallowed. "A—a dick?" she croaked. Her mind flashed to the activities of the previous evening and she felt her face flame. Was it that obvious?

"Yeah, you know. A gumshoe, a flatfoot. A dick. Truman's got a real nose for cheating spouses. He got the goods on my old man." She stepped a bit closer and lowered her voice conspiratorially. "Roy, my former scumbag husband, was bumping our next-door neighbor while I was off shaking my bootie to pay the rent. Tru caught him with his pants down and we got a quickie divorce. I got the business and the jerk took off for Florida with my neighbor." She turned and pointed to the door behind her. "Peeler's Party Strippers," she said proudly. She held out her hand. "Ruby Peeler's my name. Although my stage name is Tootie Fruitie, the Peel and Eat Treat." She ripped an apple off her right hip and handed it to Caroline. "Some of the fruit's real," she said with a giggle. "Go ahead, taste it. The guy's love to pluck it off and eat it. It's a real novelty."

Caroline glanced down at the apple. "No, thanks. I just had lunch," she murmured, handing the fruit back to Ruby. The woman shrugged and slapped the fruit back onto her hip. "I'll just wait out here for a little while, if you don't mind," Caroline said.

"Suit yourself," Ruby replied. "But sometimes Tru don't come in for days and days. He's working on a real important case now. Some big shot divorce. Hollywood producer, I think. You're welcome to wait inside my office. I don't have a professional engagement until later this afternoon. We could sit down and have a nice little girl-to-girl chat. You can tell me all about Truman and you."

Caroline shook her head. "No, that's all right. I wouldn't want to miss him if he came in."

Ruby studied her for a long moment. "You got an honest face. And I don't suppose he'd mind if I let you into his office, seeing as you're a friend and all." She pulled a ring of keys out from behind the banana on her left buttock and walked to Tru's door. "I've got keys to all the offices. The landlord goes out of town a lot so he needed a part-time building manager and I got the job. I get a pretty decent discount on the rent for doing it. If Truman don't show up, you can leave him a note. Just make sure the door locks behind you when you go."

Ruby threw the door open and Caroline slowly walked into the dim office. She turned and smiled at Ruby. "Thank you. I appreciate this."

Ruby winked. "No problem, sweetie." She reached up and withdrew a business card from behind the clump of grapes at her breast. "Here's my card. If you ever have need of a party stripper, you just give me a call. I'll give you a ten percent discount 'cause you're a friend of Truman's."

Caroline took the card and nodded. "Thanks. It was a pleasure meeting you, Ruby. And good luck with your . . . engagement." She held out her hand.

Ruby grabbed it and grinned. "The pleasure is all mine, I'm sure." With that, she turned and walked across the hall, balanced on her banana yellow five-inch high heels. Her hips swayed provocatively and the fruit wobbled with each step. As she turned to close her office door, she gave Caroline a little wave.

Caroline wiggled her fingers in return then slowly closed Tru's office door. The tiny office was stuffy, the afternoon sun beating through the closed venetian blinds. She flipped on the light switch next to the door, expecting a mess on the order of Tru's apartment. But the office was neat and tidy, as if he spent little time there. A battered antique desk sat in the middle of the room with two leather upholstered chairs in front of it. Behind the desk, file cabinets lined the wall.

She glanced around the office, looking for a clue, anything to tell her more about the man who had made love to her the night before. But there was nothing personal in the office, no pictures or knickknacks, nothing of Tru's past or present.

"I know nothing about the man," she murmured. "Except that I can't resist him."

Caroline dusted off one of the guest chairs and sat down. She was glad that he hadn't been in when she'd arrived. At least now she'd have time to collect her thoughts. All right, so she couldn't deny the attraction between them. Though she'd never recommend basing a relationship solely on sexual attraction, she was beginning to believe that this would not be a normal relationship. She and Tru would never proceed on a predictable course.

With a groan of frustration, Caroline glanced down at her watch. Impatient with the waiting, she pushed out of the chair and wandered around the tiny office. A manila file folder sitting on the corner of his immaculate desk caught her eye and she ran her finger over it. She didn't consider herself a nosy person, just curious. It was only natural to want to know more about Tru's work. She buried a pang of guilt and flipped the folder open with a flick of her nail.

Caroline drew a sharp breath and stepped back, shocked by what she found. A familiar face stared back at her from a glossy black-and-white photo. She picked up the photo and studied her image. This was not the photo of her that Tru had attempted to take in her office on the day they met. This photo had been taken at another time, in another place.

She snatched up the stack and flipped through it, a slow dread creeping up her spine. The pictures had been taken outside Ellis Stone's office building and Ellis appeared with her in a good number of the photos. She and Ellis talking, smiling, even kissing each other on the cheek. Why would Tru have photos like these in his possession? Her mind swam with possible explanations.

He had probably taken these during the time he was tracking her down. Her identity as Dr. Carly Lovelace was a well-kept secret. He would have had to put in some time searching for her. But if he'd had photos of her already, why had he attempted to take another in her office? She considered the theory for a long moment. It didn't quite make sense.

Another possibility brought a rush of panic to her throat. Maybe Tru was an obsessed fan or some kind of stalker. Maybe he was just trying to get closer to her and used the poker game as a clever and very charming excuse. Oh, Lord, she had played right into his hand, inviting him into her life, allowing him to pose as her husband. She closed her eyes and swallowed hard. Theory number two did make sense, but she had a hard time believing that Tru Hallihan was some deranged madman. He had a wicked sense of humor, but that was about as far as his lunacy went.

She drew a deep breath and calmed her nerves. Then she picked up the folder and looked at the index tag. The word *Stone* was written in a bold, masculine hand across the tab. Caroline stared at the picture of her and Ellis exchanging friendly kisses. Could Tru Hallihan be working on a case? Ruby's words came back to her. Big shot divorce. Hollywood producer. Ellis Stone?

She frowned and mulled over the evidence. It made more sense than the last two alternatives. But for whom was he working? Certainly not Ellis. Ellis was the one pictured prominently in most of the photos. It had to be Marianne!

Caroline calmly evaluated the clues she'd been given. Is that why Tru and Marianne had been so immersed in conversation at the reception? Were they plotting their strategy? And exactly how *well* did they know each other? Well enough to plan a little rendezvous at Lake Arrowhead? Caroline tried to recall all that had happened that night—Tru's surprise at finding her there, his suspicion of Ellis, his impromptu midnight wrestling match with Marianne on the couch. And the dark sedan, on the street in front of Johnny's—Tru had been watching them both, waiting to catch them in an indiscretion.

She bit back a groan and sank into one of Tru's guest chairs. It all fit. Tru was working on a divorce case for Marianne Stone, and probably sleeping with her as well. Like Marianne, he suspected Caroline of being Ellis's mistress. And to get the proof he and Marianne needed, he had wormed his way into her life, probably with Marianne's good wishes.

No, he hadn't exactly wormed. She had invited him into her life, practically handed him an engraved invitation, like some naive little fool. Well, she wasn't going to play the fool any longer. Caroline shoved the photos back into the folder and replaced them neatly on the desk, then strode to the door. As she placed her hand on the knob, footsteps thudded on the stairs outside the door.

Slowly, she backed away as a dark form appeared in the clouded glass. Holding her breath, she watched the doorknob turn. The door slowly opened and Tru stepped inside. As he looked up from his keys he stopped, surprise evident in his expression.

"Caroline."

She gulped back her anger and forced a smile. "Hello, Tru."

His gaze locked on hers as he closed the door and walked around his desk. "I got your message. I didn't expect to hear from you so soon. I hurried right over, but when I didn't see you out front, I thought I'd missed you. How did you get in?"

He tossed his keys on top of the file folder and she jumped. "Ruby let me in," she murmured. She could feel her temper bubbling out of control in her bloodstream.

He chuckled. "You met Ruby? She's quite a lady, isn't she? Remind me to thank her."

Caroline nodded curtly, then glanced down at her watch. "Oh, my," she cried, her voice tight. "Look at the time. I have to go. I've got the Hartmanns coming in at two and the Sampsons at three." She rushed to the door.

In three quick steps, he joined her there, grabbing her by the elbow and pulling her to a stop. "Wait a second," he said. "Aren't you going to tell me why you wanted to meet me here?" The touch of his fingers on her arm was like an electric shock, sending a tingle right to her toes and weakening her knees.

"No!" she snapped. "I mean, it's not important. It will keep. I really have to run now. I'll call you and we'll talk . . . later." She pulled out of his grasp and stumbled down the stairs.

"Caroline!" he called. "Come back here. What the hell is going on?"

"I'm late!" she replied. The front door slammed behind her and she scurried down the street to her car, half expecting him to follow her. She glanced in the rearview mirror the instant before she pulled out into traffic. He stood in front of his office building, watching her, but not pursuing. She kept looking back at his reflection until she turned off at the next intersection.

Her grip loosened on the wheel and she forced back a flood of tears. His deception had blindsided her, knocking the breath from her until she felt as if she'd never draw another. Everything between them had been an act. He had tricked her and she had fallen right into his slimy little trap.

And on the way, she made a short detour into his bed as well.

"HOW HARD can it possibly be?" Caroline asked sarcastically. "*Tru Hallihan* does it for a living, after all. And I've studied this book from cover to cover." She picked up the book from her desk and handed it to Aurora.

"*Private Investigating Made Easy?*" Aurora asked. She looked at the back cover. "A ten-step program to a new career in the exciting world of private investigations. Caro, I know how much faith you put in self-improvement, but this is taking it a little too far. You can't learn to be a private investigator from a book."

"We *can* learn from a book," Caroline corrected. "And we will."

"Oh, no," Aurora protested. "I'm not helping you with this."

"But you have to! Your psychic powers will be a big help. Gut instinct is an important quality in a good P.I. Chapter six."

"Gut instinct?"

"Right. Gut instinct, intuition, psychic powers. It's all the same, isn't it?"

Aurora smiled indulgently. "My powers have nothing at all to do with . . . guts."

"And the book says I'm going to need a partner." Caroline opened the manual and flipped through the pages. "Here it is. Chapter four. Surveillance work in a vehicle is made easier with the help of a partner. One person can drive while the other keeps a close eye on the subject. We also need to use your car. A five-year-old Toyota hatchback makes a better plain wrapper than my BMW. A plain wrapper means—"

"I can imagine what it means," Aurora said. "Let me get this straight. We're going to use my...wrapper to follow Tru Hallihan?"

"We are not only going to follow Tru Hallihan, we're going to give him a taste of his own medicine. We're going to catch *him* with his pants down," Caroline said, a bitter edge to her voice.

"Sounds very interesting," Aurora said. "And this is what we need the camera for? To photograph him without his pants?" Her lips curled into a smile. "Maybe this doesn't sound so bad."

"We're going to catch him trying to catch Ellis Stone. And if we're lucky, we may even catch him in the act of perpetrating an extramarital infidelity," Caroline explained.

The thought of finding Tru Hallihan in bed with another woman, especially Marianne Stone, caused a sharp pain to twist at Caroline's heart. She steeled herself against her feelings. Tru had betrayed her, had played her for the fool. And now she was about to even the score. In the process, she'd find the crucial sense of closure she so badly needed for this sordid episode in her life. "We aren't *actually* going to catch him with his pants down, though. Can you get Darrell's camera?"

"Caroline, I haven't agreed to help you with this yet. Never mind the fact that I'd have to pretend to be a private investigator, but I'm not getting up at six in the morning just to sit in front of Tru Hallihan's apartment building and wait for him to come out. Not without a good reason."

"It's the only way this will work. We have to . . ." She frantically riffled through the book and found the pertinent page. ". . . to catch his tail early in the day, or we'll never find him. Come on. Darrell is out of town at that video game convention and I need your help. Besides, if I don't get the goods on Tru Hallihan, I might as well forget my television show. I've got to give Ellis at least a chance to even the odds."

"Is this really about Ellis?" Aurora asked. "Or is it about you?"

"I don't know what you mean," she answered, crossing her arms in a defensive posture.

"What happened between the two of you? I mean, besides the obvious."

Caroline forced a bland expression. "The obvious?"

"You made love to him, Caroline," Aurora said softly.

"I did not!" she cried.

"Don't lie to me. I can see it in your eyes."

"It wasn't love," Caroline replied. "We had sex. It was all a lie, a deception, a trick. Tru Hallihan has been . . . undercover, so to speak. Trying to collect evidence to use against Ellis Stone in a divorce case. And along the way, he decided to use me to get what he needed."

"Have you confronted Tru about this? Have you given him a chance to explain?"

"I don't need his explanations," she replied stubbornly. "Right now, I need closure." She paused. "And just a little bit of revenge."

"Honest communication is the cornerstone of any successful relationship," Aurora stated.

"Tell that to Mr. Hallihan. And we don't have a relationship. We had a night in bed. That doesn't constitute a relationship. It constitutes an incident. An unfortunate incident."

"You can say it easily enough. But it's a little hard to believe it, isn't it?"

Caroline shot her an exasperated look. "If you don't stop that, I'm going to find myself a lead helmet. There are times when I'd prefer to keep my thoughts to myself."

"I've told you a million times, I can't always read your mind like the morning paper. I'm a psychic, Caroline, with some sporadic telepathic powers. And I'm your friend. I know when something's hurting you and I only want to help."

"If you're my friend, then help me with this. I can't risk Tru Hallihan ruining my chances for this television show. We have to find a way to stop him. Ellis Stone told me he's innocent of any infidelity and I believe him. And if Hallihan tries to prove otherwise, we'll have something to fight him with."

Aurora sighed. "All right. I'll help. But only if you promise me something."

"What?" Caroline asked.

"After you find whatever it is you're looking for, I want you to promise to at least talk to Tru Hallihan and get his side of the story."

"Oh, I'll talk to him all right," Caroline muttered. She walked over to the small closet in her office and opened the door, then pulled out a trench coat. "Here. This is for you. Standard uniform." Caroline handed Aurora the beige coat, then pulled a pair of sunglasses and a dark cap out of the pocket.

Aurora stared at the coat distastefully. "No way, Caro! You know very well that I'm allergic to beige."

"I'm afraid they don't make bright purple trench coats, Aurora, so you'll just have to make do. And I want you to put your hair up under that cap. I'll pick you up tomorrow morning at six a.m. sharp. Tru sleeps late so I don't think we'll see much action before eight or nine."

"I'll bring the croissants and café lattes," Aurora volunteered. "And I'll have Elly's Deli make up a few of those gourmet box lunches for us. They make the best crab salad and they put it on their special veggie bread. And I'll pick up a six-pack of that kiwi-mango drink that you like so much. And some of those killer brownies."

"This isn't a picnic, Aurora."

"Does the book require that we private eyes subsist on a diet of stale donuts and muddy coffee? Does the book require that we have to ignore good taste and proper nutrition?"

"I guess not," Caroline replied. She opened the book and flipped to the correct page. "The book says we should also bring along newspapers, sunglasses, hats, a roll of quarters for the parking meters, a camera, binoculars, paper and pencil, and a wide-mouthed bottle."

"A wide-mouthed bottle. What for?"

Caroline skimmed down the page. "I don't know, I guess for—" She stopped and gaped at the answer.

"What?" Aurora asked.

Caroline crinkled her nose. "Let's just say you and I will be using the ladies' room at the nearest fast-food restaurant whenever necessary," she replied.

HE CAUGHT the dark blue sedan tailing him shortly after he'd pulled out of his parking spot at the Bachelor Arms. Tru made a few lazy turns to be sure. The car followed at a steady distance. Whoever was tailing him was obviously an amateur. He'd made the dolt in the Toyota in less than ten blocks, a new record in his book.

He slowed his drive through rush hour traffic, making sure the Toyota didn't lose him. As he wound through the streets of West Hollywood, he tried to figure out who had put a tail on him. After fifteen minutes of mentally flipping through his recent case files without an answer, Tru decided to find out for himself.

"Whoever you are," he muttered, "you don't know squat about surveillance."

He pulled up in front of a small greasy spoon, taking his time to park. The Toyota pulled in a few cars behind him, in front of a dry cleaners. Tru stepped from his car, acting as oblivious to the tail as possible but catching a glimpse of the two passengers from behind his Ray-Bans. Baseball caps, dark glasses. He stepped inside the diner and continued to covertly watch them through the front window.

When neither driver nor passenger got out after ten minutes, Tru walked through the restaurant kitchen and out the rear door. He headed down to the dry cleaners and slipped in the back door, then made his way through the store, weaving around baffled employees and racks of plastic-draped clothes. He had a perfect view of the car through the plate glass window.

The sight of Caroline's perfect profile, hidden behind the dark glasses and the low brim of a Dodger cap, came as a complete surprise to him. He chuckled and shook his head. What the hell was she up to? And who the hell was she up to it with?

He slid his sunglasses down on his nose and studied the driver. Another woman. No one he recognized. The pair was so intent on watching the entrance to the restaurant, they didn't see him sneak out the front door of the dry cleaners and read the rear plate on the Toyota.

A minute later, he was back inside the restaurant, placing a call to his buddy at the Highway Patrol. He'd call him back from his next stop for the I.D. on the registration. Tru grabbed a cup of coffee and a cheese Danish before he made a show of leaving the greasy spoon.

He'd planned to spend the morning at the office finishing up the paperwork on the Stone case before dropping his report at Marshall Enterprises. Simon Marshall wouldn't be happy, but Tru had uncovered no solid evidence of Ellis Stone's infidelity. And he wanted to rid himself of the case, and its twenty-thousand-dollar temptation as soon as he could. It was the only threat to a solid future with Caroline and if he was lucky, she'd never find out about the job, and he'd never have a reason to tell her.

But paperwork was a dead bore compared to having a little fun with Caroline Leighton, rookie private investigator, and her wheelwoman. He clamped the Danish between his teeth and pulled open the car door, then hopped inside and slowly maneuvered out into traffic. His next stop was the car wash. He cranked the roof up on the Caddy and ran it through the automatic wash twice. Much to his amusement, the Toyota followed him through both times. While he waited for them to finish their second wash and wax, he called and got the registration on the Toyota. Aurora Starr owned the car.

After a painfully slow drive down Santa Monica Boulevard, Tru's next stop was Venice Beach. He parked the Caddy and got out to stroll the oceanfront walk.

Caroline and her friend, Aurora, seemed hesitant to follow, but finally climbed out of the car and shadowed him at a discreet distance. They looked like a pair of flashers, completely out of place in their trench coats, wandering among the colorfully and scantily garbed in-line skaters and bodybuilders. They'd almost lost him in the crowd a few times, until he stopped to buy a wild tiger-striped cap from a street vendor. With the cap on his head, they'd have to be blind not to see him.

Stop number three on Tru's ten-cent tour of Los Angeles—Hollywood Boulevard. He was surprised when Caroline got out of the car. The tawdry atmosphere of the street was more than a little frightening, especially to someone used to strolling Rodeo Drive. But the street was safe enough in daylight. She followed him along the Walk of Fame. He set a brisk pace, and when he couldn't hear her footsteps behind him, he stopped suddenly and turned to look into a shop window. Caroline darted for cover. He continued down the sidewalk, smiling to himself and repeating the action over and over again until he was certain she was ready to scream in frustration.

His final test of Caroline's determination came when he turned into the garishly lit door of a topless bar. Once inside the darkened interior he could watch her through the glass door without being seen. She walked by the bar three times and loitered outside for nearly ten minutes before she decided to venture in.

He was about to confront her, unwilling to put her safety at risk in the seedy strip joint, but when he glanced around, he found the bar nearly empty. A bartender with a face like a ferret watched him from behind a cloud of cigar smoke. On the long runway, a voluptuous dancer in a G-string and pasties shimmied lethargically to ear-numbing music. The only patron, a sleeping drunk, snored at a stage-side table.

Tru smiled smugly and pulled off the flashy cap, then placed it snugly on the drunk's head. He found a dark corner at the bar to watch the action unfold. Caroline entered a few moments later and spotted the cap immediately, snapping at the bait like a starving bluefin. She took a seat at one of the tables behind the drunk, slouching down in her chair and trying to look as inconspicuous as possible.

She hadn't bothered to survey the rest of the bar, so intent was she on the cap and the man beneath it. Tru motioned the bartender over and slipped him two twenties, then whispered a careful set of instructions. With a shrug, the bartender accepted his assignment and stepped out from behind the bar. He approached Caroline to take a drink order and Tru could hear his booming voice above the blasting music.

"Whadda ya want, missy?" the bartender yelled.

Caroline shrank in her seat at his words, then shook her head, trying to deflect attention from herself. She was obviously concerned about drawing Tru's notice, but the drunk she'd taken for him was out for the count. He wouldn't be moving before the late show.

"Ya wanna watch, ya gotta drink," Ferret-Face said.

She ordered a drink and dug some money out of her coat pocket, then adjusted her sunglasses and tugged on her cap.

"We ain't got no diet soda," the bartender shouted. "Whadda ya think this is, lady, some fancy fern bar?"

Tru chuckled softly at the grimace on Caroline's face. Though she was enormously uncomfortable, she had resolved to tough it out. He had to admire her nerve, misplaced as it might be.

Throughout his impromptu tour of the area's highlights and lowlights, he'd tried to figure out what might possess her to follow him. She knew what he did for a living, he'd made no secret of his profession. In fact, except for the Stone case, he had no secrets at all. Nothing to hide from her. No girlfriends, no sleazy life-style or criminal record.

Tru frowned. There was no way she could know about the case, was there? He'd covered his tracks well . . . or had he? His mind snapped back to her strange behavior at his office. Could she have stumbled onto something there that had tipped her off? He brushed away the notion. If she had, why hadn't she confronted him then and there? When it came to honest communication, Caroline never wasted time thinking before she spoke.

He took a gulp of his flat club soda and shook his head. There was no use trying to read her mind. He'd just have to play this little cat-and-mouse game out to the end. And hope she'd give him a clue somewhere along the way.

Tru watched as she gave the bartender another order. The man chomped on his cigar and nodded in reply. On his way back to the bar, he ambled past the stage and muttered into the dancer's ear, pressing Tru's twenty into her hand.

Though Tru was tempted to put Caroline out of her misery, he waited patiently for the grand finale. As the next number blasted out of the speakers, the dancer shuffled down the stage steps and headed toward Caroline's table. Once there, she began an enthusiastic bump and grind, shimmying and shaking until Caroline had no choice but to bury her face in her hands.

Only then did Tru slip off his bar stool and walk over to her table. With her eyes covered, she was unaware of his approach. He stood behind her and bent down next to her ear. "She's not *that* bad," he said. "Maybe she'd consider giving you lessons."

Her hands came off her eyes in an instant and she turned and looked up at him. She snatched off her sunglasses and blinked until her vision adjusted to the change in light. "You!" she cried. Realization slowly dawned on her flushed face. "You knew we were following you. You set this all up!"

He pulled out a chair and sat down next to her, then waved the dancer off. "If I were you," he shouted over the music. "I wouldn't give up your regular job. You and your friend weren't cut out for surveillance work. A city bus with lights flashing and the horn blowing would have been less obvious."

"Oh, yeah? Well, don't be so sure about that. It didn't take much to find out what you were really up to," she said angrily.

He glanced around the room and shrugged. "This? You don't like my choice of afternoon entertainment?"

"That's not what I'm talking about," she yelled.

He grabbed her hand playfully, but she yanked it away. Her expression was icy cold and emotionless. A flicker of concern licked like a flame at his gut. "All right," he said. "I give up. What *are* you talking about?"

"When were you planning to tell me about your investigation of Ellis Stone?"

The flame extinguished as his stomach dropped to his feet at light speed. He ground his teeth and cursed his luck. Damn, she knew. How she knew, he wasn't sure. But she knew. "How did you find out?"

"It doesn't matter. Answer me," she demanded.

"I wasn't going to tell you," he muttered.

"What?" she shouted, above the din of the music.

"I wasn't going to tell you!" he replied. "My clients are protected by a code of confidentiality."

She shot up from her seat. "That's just great!" She laughed caustically. "You planned to destroy my television career, my dreams, without blinking an eye and then, in the next second, hop right into bed with me. And then you planned to hide behind some damn private eye code. What a wonderful start to a long and loving relationship. I'm so glad you decided to forget your ethical standards and be honest with me." With that, she ripped off her cap and stalked toward the door, her hair tumbled wildly around her face.

"That's not the way it is, Caroline," he shouted after her.

She shoved against the door and stepped out onto the street. He followed on her heels, weaving through the bikers and the punks and the rest of the riffraff that swarmed along Hollywood Boulevard. He managed to pull her to a stop on top of Esther Williams's star.

"Let me go!" she hissed. "I have nothing to say to you." She slipped out of his grasp and continued down the street.

"Caroline, I wasn't going to tell you, because there was nothing to tell. I dropped the case."

He grabbed her sleeve again, and she gave him an elbow in the gut. "Dammit, Caroline, listen to me. I dropped the case. I'm going to tell Simon Marshall that I didn't find any proof of infidelity."

She stopped and spun around to face him. "Who's Simon Marshall?"

"He's Ellis's father-in-law. He's the one who hired me. He offered me twenty thousand dollars to prove grounds on Ellis. And if I succeeded, he was going to put me on retainer with his corporation, doing background checks on potential employees. I didn't find anything. And that's what I'm going to tell him. That's the truth, Caroline."

Tears flooded her eyes and she shook her head. "How am I supposed to believe anything you say? You've been lying to me all along."

"This is the truth. I swear."

She forced a wavering smile though her tears. "The truth. You know, I always questioned my sanity when I was around you. My attraction to you was totally illogical. We had nothing in common, nothing to build on." She sniffed and wiped at her cheeks. "Except maybe honesty. And now, we don't have that, either. I must have been crazy to think we had a future."

He reached out to her but she stepped back. "I'm being honest now, Caroline. I love you. You have to believe that. I wouldn't do anything to hurt you." The words came so easily, words he had never thought he would say... or mean. But he did love her, he was certain of it.

She drew a shaky breath and tipped up her chin in that sweetly stubborn way of hers, as if she were discounting his proclamation as just another lie. "You already have. I've made my decision, Tru."

The look of despondency on her face stabbed through him like a knife.

"We don't have a future," she said softly. "I don't want you. And I—I don't love you."

The knife twisted, the searing pain stealing the breath from his chest.

"Goodbye, Tru." She turned and started toward her friend's car. Stunned, Tru muttered a vivid curse and raked his hands through his hair as he watched her walk down the street. Past the pizza parlors and the souvenir shops, past the X-rated bookstores and strip joints. The only woman he had ever loved was walking right out of his life, and there was nothing he could do or say to stop her.

# 9

THE RECLINER WAS JAMMED squarely in the doorway of Tru's apartment. Garrett and Josh were inside, shoving against the back of the chair with their shoulders. Tru stood in the hallway and watched. The harder they pushed, the more firmly wedged the chair became.

"It's not moving, Hallihan," Garrett growled. "How the hell did you get the damn thing through the door the first time?"

Tru shrugged. "I don't remember. Maybe it was here when I moved in." He stared at the chair for a long moment, then crawled over top of it into his apartment. "Maybe we need a break to reevaluate our strategy. I don't think this plan is working."

"Maybe we need a chain saw," Garrett muttered.

"There is a solution to this problem," Josh murmured. "It's all a matter of geometry." He pulled out a tape measure and began to survey the dimensions of the chair.

Tru wandered into the kitchen and returned with three beers. He tossed one to Garrett and set the other on the arm of the recliner, not willing to disturb Josh's precise calculations.

"I don't know why you're moving in the first place," Garrett said as he flopped down on the couch. "You couldn't pay me enough to live in spook central."

"Amberson needs a tenant in 1-G and I want a bigger place. The only bad thing about all those rumors is that it hasn't lowered the rent. You'd think I'd at least get a break for letting the lady in the mirror live with me."

"You mean you're not taking the mirror down?" Garrett asked.

"Amberson says it doesn't come off the wall. I'm not sure if that means it isn't possible or it isn't allowed, but I'm not going to argue with him. Besides, I've already seen the lady. She won't be back."

Garrett's gaze snapped up from the magazine he was flipping through. "You've seen her?"

"Clear as day," Tru said.

"Give me a break. You don't expect me to believe that, do you?"

"Believe it or not, I don't care. It's the truth. It was about six or seven weeks ago," he said. "Right after I met Caroline Leighton," Tru added distractedly.

"Caroline Leighton. You mean Carly Lovelace?"

Tru nodded. Even the sound of her name affected him, bringing back a rush of sensations. He could still hear her voice, recall it in an instant, even though he had avoided listening to her show since they had parted. And he remembered the scent of her hair and the vivid green of her eyes, little things that suddenly seemed so important to him.

"So, tell me, was she your dream or your nightmare?" Garrett joked.

Tru shook his head and grabbed a box of books. "The hell if I know. I've been trying to figure that one out myself." Over the past four weeks he'd done little else. He thought it would be easy to forget her, but with every day that passed, he became more certain she was not going to go away. And with every night, his fears were proved. She appeared in his dreams, soft and seductive. He'd wake up and she wouldn't be there, and he'd pace his apartment until his arousal diminished and exhaustion took over. She had carved out a place for herself in his heart and evicting her would only leave a painful, gaping hole.

Tru climbed back over the chair and took the tape measure from Josh's hands. "Come on, Josh. Maybe if you leave it alone, it will squeeze through on its own," he said. "We'll be back in a few minutes, McCabe. Why don't you work on a solution that doesn't include power tools."

Josh distractedly grabbed a box and followed Tru over the chair. "It sounds like Caroline Leighton really got to you," Josh commented softly as he joined Tru in the hall.

Tru glanced over at him in surprise. He hadn't realized that Josh had been listening. "Yeah," he admitted, "she got to me. I was in love with her. I still am."

He couldn't count the number of times he had picked up the phone, intending to call her, or the times he had been tempted to stop by her office and force her to talk to him. Then he would recall their last minutes together, her stinging rejection, and he would bury the urge. But no matter how deeply he buried it, the need to see her again never really went away.

Josh frowned. "You're in love with her?"

Tru nodded.

"Then why aren't you with her?" Josh asked in his strangely direct way.

Tru paused a long moment and then smiled. "I don't know. Maybe I should be."

"That would make sense considering your feelings," Josh said.

They walked silently down the stairs and through the hall to apartment 1-G. Most of Tru's belongings had already been moved, including his bookcases. All that was left upstairs was the studio couch and the recliner and the meager contents of the refrigerator. Tru unlocked the door and walked inside.

Every time he walked in, he couldn't help but remember the first day he'd seen the apartment. He dropped the box on the floor and crossed over to the mirror, then stood and stared at it, waiting. But the only thing that stared back was his own reflection. His jaw was shadowed with a week-old beard. He looked thinner than usual and there were dark circles under his eyes from lack of sleep. Tru raked his hands through his hair, then turned away. He grabbed the box he'd brought down and began to shelve his collection of detective novels.

"Garrett says you need to get back in the saddle," Josh commented. "I assume he means that you should take your mind off of your problems with Caroline by dating someone else."

Tru shook his head. "I'm not really in the mood," he said, flipping through a yellowed copy of *The Maltese Falcon.* He hadn't read the book in years. Maybe it was time to find some consolation in his old friends. He grabbed a dog-eared copy of Spillane's *Vengeance Is Mine* and skimmed the first page.

He remembered the first time he'd read the novel. He couldn't have been more than eleven or twelve. He'd found it at a thrift shop and liked the title. It had cost him a nickel. A nickel that had changed his life. A nickel to soothe the ache of his mother's absence and his father's distance. "I've got some paperwork to take care of at the office and some reading to do."

"Avoiding your problems and feeling sorry for yourself won't help," Josh said.

Tru turned to him in irritation. He was tired and edgy and at any other time, he would have laughed off his friend's comment. But Josh had come too close to the truth this time. "Maybe I am avoiding the problem," Tru admitted. "But right now, feeling sorry for myself is the only thing I want to do."

Josh wandered over and pulled one of the detective novels from the box. "If you really love her, I can think of a lot better ways to spend your time."

"What would you suggest?" Tru asked.

"Call her," Josh said, placing the book on the shelf. "Go to see her. Send her flowers. Write her poems. Show her how you feel and don't give up until you've got her back."

Tru stared at his friend in disbelief. Josh had never offered advice in the past. He usually only observed silently when the conversation turned to women. "Josh, do you know what you're talking about or are you just making this up as you go along?"

"I know that you won't get her back by doing what you're doing now—nothing." Josh walked across the room and stood in front of the mirror. "In situations like these it is best to take a proactive approach."

"You think I should try to get her back?" Tru asked.

"Definitely," he said, staring at his reflection. Tru watched as Josh held up his arm at a right angle and clenched his fist, then carefully examined his bicep.

"She's not going to want to see me," Tru countered.

"Doesn't make any difference," Josh said as he examined the pewter frame.

"But she said—"

"If you've found someone you really want to spend your life with, consider yourself lucky," Josh interrupted. "And don't let anything stand in your way."

A tiny thread of hope wove its way through Tru's mind. Maybe he could get her back. Maybe he could convince her to forget the past and start all over again. Gut instinct told him that she cared about him, that it had been as hard for her to walk away as it had been for him to watch. He wouldn't know how she really felt unless he tried.

"Garrett says they're taping her show tomorrow afternoon," Josh offered. "Maybe you should go down there and talk to her."

Tru grinned. "Maybe I should," he said. "Maybe I will." Tru shoved the rest of the books haphazardly on the shelf. "Come on, let's go see if McCabe has had any luck with that chair."

Tru started for the door, but when Josh didn't follow he turned back to find his friend still standing in front of the mirror, transfixed by his own reflection.

"Hey, are you coming?"

Josh was silent, a perplexed frown on his face.

Tru walked over to him and tapped him on the shoulder. "Josh?"

Josh jumped, startled by Tru's touch.

"Are you all right?" Tru asked.

Josh turned to him, a confused expression on his face. "Yeah," he said. "Sure. I'm fine. Let's go."

Tru smiled. "You sure you're all right?"

"Yeah," Josh insisted.

Tru grabbed an empty box and shoved it at Josh. "Then, come on, Banks. Move it. I've got places to go and a lady to woo. And there's a BarcaLounger recliner standing in my way."

An hour later, freshly showered and shaved, Tru wound his way through the streets of downtown L.A. He found the offices for Marshall Enterprises and parked the Caddy on the street. The security guard in the lobby gave him only a lazy glance as he passed by on his way to the elevators. The receptionist outside Marshall's office was not as easy.

"No, I don't have an appointment," Tru said. "Just tell Mr. Marshall that Tru Hallihan is here to see him."

The receptionist gave him a look that could sour milk. "I'm afraid that Mr. Marshall doesn't see anyone without an appointment," she said, her voice professional, yet patronizing.

"He'll see me," Tru assured her. "Just tell him."

With a sniff, she snatched up her phone and buzzed the inner office. Ten seconds later, he was politely led down a long hall to a set of mahogany doors. Marshall stood as Tru entered the room, an expectant smile splitting his florid face.

"Hallihan!" Marshall cried. "Good to see you. Please, take a seat. Can Louise get you anything to drink?"

After hearing what he had come to say, Tru was certain that Marshall would pull the welcome mat right out from under his feet. Simon Marshall was not going to be happy with the results of Tru's investigation. But he'd get over it—eventually. Maybe he'd even decide to quit meddling in his daughter's marriage.

Tru threw his report onto Marshall's desk. "I won't have time for coffee," he replied. "There's the report. I didn't find anything. As far as I could tell, your son-in-law isn't cheating on his wife."

Marshall's features slowly frosted over. He sat down at his desk and studied Tru with a shrewd gaze. "I hired you to do a job, Hallihan. I hired you to *find* the proof."

"If you're implying you expected me to fabricate evidence, then you came to the wrong man."

"I can see that," Marshall said bitterly.

Tru placed his palms on Marshall's desk and leaned across the smoothly polished surface. "I'm a professional investigator, Mr. Marshall, and though there are a lot of unscrupulous P.I.s in this business, I'm not one of them. You asked me to investigate Ellis Stone and I did. I found nothing to indicate infidelity. And twenty thousand dollars is not enough to compromise my professional integrity."

"If you don't want the twenty thousand, I'm sure I'll be able to find someone who does," Marshall said.

"Let me give you a little bit of advice, Simon. Stay out of your daughter's marriage. Ellis Stone is a good man and he loves your daughter. Don't make her choose between the two of you. You might just find yourself out in the cold."

Tru turned and walked toward the door, but Marshall's next comment stopped him.

"I really thought you could do the job, Hallihan. But I guess it's your loss, isn't it?"

He slowly turned back to Marshall. "You had a chance to hire me and I'm the best. I'm fair and I'm honest and I would have done a good job for you." Tru pulled the door open. "Oh, by the way, if I were you, I'd fire that security guard downstairs. And I'd invest in lobby and elevator cameras. And when your receptionist brought me in here, she left her computer unattended. A good hacker can crack a system in a matter of minutes. Whoever's in charge of your security isn't doing a very good job. I'd definitely say that was *your* loss now, wouldn't you?"

With that Tru stepped through the door, leaving Simon Marshall dumbfounded. He heard the man bellow his name as he walked down the hall, but he didn't stop. As Tru passed the receptionist, he handed her his card.

"He'll be asking for my number," Tru said. "Let him know I'll be in my office tomorrow morning. We can discuss his security problems at that time."

CAROLINE PACED the length of the tiny dressing room, staring down at the black studded shoes.

Aurora studied her from a chair. Her legs were thrown over the arm and she had her ever-present tarot cards in her hand. She shuffled them idly. "You can't wear those," she said. "They don't match."

"I don't care," Caroline replied. "I want to wear these shoes. I need to wear these shoes. Now find me a suit that goes with them. I brought seven choices along."

"Caro, the only suit that would go with those shoes would involve skin-tight leather and fishnet stockings," Aurora said. "Not appropriate wardrobe for afternoon television."

"Carly Lovelace would wear these shoes," Caroline explained. "And I'm Carly Lovelace, so I'm going to wear them."

"Then the red suit is your best bet," Aurora advised.

"The red? Do you really think so?" Caroline asked.

"Yes, I *really* think so. Now, put on the suit and relax. You're beginning to make *me* nervous."

"Do I look nervous?" Caroline asked desperately. "I don't want to appear nervous. But I feel nervous. I shouldn't feel nervous. I'm well prepared, I've interviewed the couple, I know exactly what I'm going to say, and I—"

"Sit!" Aurora ordered.

Caroline slid into the other chair and watched her friend. "I told several of my patients about the show," she admitted, picking idly at an imaginary piece of lint on her sleeve. "And they said that they'd like to remain with me if I had time to see them."

"That's nice," Aurora said as she flipped through the tarot cards.

"And I called my parents and told them. They weren't happy, but they were properly supportive. I'm sure they'll come around sooner or later. So, you see, there's really no reason for me to be nervous and I—"

Aurora stopped at one card and stared at it long and hard, gnawing on a purple-painted fingernail, her brow furrowed.

"What?" Caroline asked. "What do you see in the cards? Tell me, is it bad?"

"You don't believe in the cards," Aurora said.

"Right now, I'm ready to believe in anything. Please, tell me."

Aurora smiled and she held up a card. "Knight of Swords," she said. "It came up in the sixth position."

"The sixth position? What does that mean? Is that bad?"

"No, it's not bad. Usually I lay the cards out on a table in a Celtic cross, but I don't have a table, so I read them this way. This card would have fallen on the sixth position. This card tells me what is before you. Things that will come to pass in the near future."

"I'm going to see a knight with a sword riding a horse?" Caroline asked.

Aurora chuckled and shook her head. "The Knight of Swords represents a dashing, brave man. Dark of hair, dark of eyes. The knight may be domineering, but he has a true heart and he will not give up."

"A true heart," Caroline murmured. She closed her eyes and slumped back into the chair. "Don't tell me. Tru Hallihan, right?"

"I'd interpret it that way," Aurora said.

"Isn't there any other way you could interpret it?" she asked.

"Sometimes the card means the coming of misfortune. Sometimes the end of bad things. But that's not what I think it means. I think you'll be seeing Tru Hallihan again, very soon."

Caroline covered her face with her hands. "When? Will he just show up on my doorstep or will he call? How is this going to happen?"

Aurora shook her head. "I don't know. Maybe you'll call him?"

"No," Caroline said decisively, sitting upright in the chair. "Forget it. I don't care what your cards say, I'm not getting myself involved with Tru Hallihan again."

"But you love him," Aurora said.

Caroline's fingers twisted nervously on her lap and her palms were damp. "Sometimes that's not enough. Believe me, I've gone over this a million times in my mind. I've made hundreds of lists, weighed all the factors, and I keep coming up with the same thing. Tru and I can never have a relationship."

"But you love him," Aurora repeated.

"Yes," she admitted with a reluctant sigh. "I love him. And someday, I hope that feeling will fade. But for now, I just have to move on with my life and forget him."

"That might not be so easy," Aurora said.

"Why not? I'm a practical person, I know what's best for me and it's not Tru Hallihan. Sooner or later someone else will come along and I'll forget all about him." The words sounded false even to her.

"You're forgetting about cosmic destiny," Aurora said.

"Cosmic destiny," Caroline repeated. Maybe it was her destiny to never find another man quite like Tru. Maybe every time she found a man, it would be her destiny to know that he paled in comparison to Tru. He was her . . . her Knight of Swords, dark and demanding, passionate and compelling. And destiny be damned, she knew she'd never love a man the way she loved him.

A knock on the door shook her out of her reverie. Aurora pushed out of her chair and went to answer it.

"I'd like to speak to Dr. Leighton."

Caroline turned and watched as Marianne Stone walked into the dressing room. She quickly stood and forced a smile. "Marianne. How are you?"

Marianne shifted uneasily and glanced back at Aurora, her gaze focusing on Aurora's crazy hairstyle. She arched a perfect brow. "I'm fine," she said, turning back to Caroline. "Could we talk? Alone?"

"Hey, no problem," Aurora said. "I'll be down the hall in makeup. You're due there in another ten minutes, Dr. Lovelace." She flipped her hair over her shoulder with a jangle of bracelets. "Maybe they can give me some beauty tips on my hair. I can't seem to do a *thing* with it." She waltzed out of the room, making a nasty face and two cat claws at Marianne's back before she closed the door.

"Please, sit down," Caroline said, pointing to a chair.

"I'd rather stand," she replied, an icy edge to her voice. "I just have a few things to say."

A shiver of apprehension shot through Caroline. She didn't need this. Not today, of all days. If Marianne was here to start something, she'd just have to walk out.

"What is it?" Caroline asked, masking her mistrust with a detached "doctor" voice.

"First, I want to apologize," Marianne said. "For my behavior toward your husband. I was out of line and I'm sorry if I caused any problems between the two of you."

Caroline controlled her surprise. She could see what the apology was costing Marianne, how it pricked her considerable pride. "I can understand your behavior," Caroline said. "You were upset and you wanted to strike back at your husband. And at the person you thought was responsible for your marital troubles."

"I know he wasn't having an affair with you," she stated.

"No, he wasn't," Caroline said softly.

Marianne drew a deep breath. "Ellis tells me that you've recommended we see a marriage counselor."

"I think it's the only way to solve your problems. Ellis loves you, Marianne. And he doesn't want to lose you. But I think you have to try to get to the root of your problems and your insecurities. You need to find those things that made you fall in love with him in the first place. And then you need to focus on that love. That's what will see you through this rough spot."

Marianne's icy expression suddenly melted. She bit her trembling lower lip and her gaze dropped to her shoes. "I do love him," Marianne admitted. "I think that's why I've been so crazy. I couldn't bear the thought that he might be happy with another woman."

Caroline bent down and caught her gaze. "Sometimes little things get blown out of proportion, an angry comment here, a stray look there. We make mistakes in our interpretations. If you learn to communicate, honestly and openly, you'll always know the truth."

Marianne smiled weakly. "You don't know how jealous I was of you."

"Because I was spending time with Ellis?" Caroline asked.

"No, because you had a good marriage. You and Lance are so much like Ellis and me, yet you seemed so suited for each other, so happy. You had gotten past the money and the career issues. I could see that he loved you and that he'd make sure you never doubted that love, and that made me envious."

Caroline sighed. How could she possibly continue the charade, especially when Marianne was opening up her heart? It was cruel and unethical. And what difference would it make? They weren't about to send the audience home. She'd get her shot either way. "Marianne, Lance and I have had our problems. We don't have a perfect…marriage. In fact, we don't have a marriage at all."

Marianne's brow wrinkled in confusion. "What do you mean?"

"It's a long story and one I should have told you and Ellis from the start. I'm not married. I was, but my husband divorced me three years ago. I was worried that Ellis and the syndicate executives might not want to take a chance on a marriage counselor whose only failure was her own marriage. Lance isn't really my husband, in fact, his name isn't even Lance. He's just a guy who agreed to pretend to be my husband as part of a poker bet. You can tell Ellis if you want. But I'm planning to tell him myself after the show. I just hope he won't be angry."

Marianne stared at Caroline for a long moment before she let out a hearty laugh. "Caroline, don't be naive. You're the star of his new daytime project. You're holding all the cards. Ellis won't be angry, believe me. You could be a convicted felon, and neither he nor the syndicate executive would care, as long as you deliver your demographic." Marianne paused then grinned again. "You got your 'husband' in a poker bet?"

"Yes," Caroline replied.

"Ellis and I met on a bet," she said. "We were both attending a premiere party. I was a real party girl and Ellis was working some entry-level job with the movie company. One of his friends bet him that he couldn't get a date with me. He was so sweet and so charming. And handsome, but not nearly as handsome as he is today. I think I fell in love with him right on the spot."

"I think I fell in love with Tru the minute I saw him," Caroline said. "I just didn't know it. It took me a while to realize what was happening."

"Tru?"

"That's his name. Short for Truman. He just bulldozed his way into my life. He's nothing like the man I expected to fall in love with."

"Ellis wasn't either. I guess that's why it was so easy to push him away, to assume that we'd made a mistake. But you're right about going back to the basics. I remember how Ellis made me feel that first night. That's what's important."

"Yes," Caroline murmured, her mind recalling her own feelings about Tru. "That's what's important."

"I—I was hoping that Ellis and I might come to see you instead of the other counselor. To work out our problems. You understand what's gone on between us and I'd feel better talking to you about it. And once your show goes into regular production, you won't be dealing with Ellis that much, so it wouldn't be a conflict of interest."

Caroline smiled. "I'd be happy to help you. Why don't you call my office and we'll set up an appointment."

A look of relief suffused Marianne's lovely face. "Thank you. For everything. And I won't tell Ellis about your marriage. Maybe there isn't any need to. And your audience won't need to know, at least, not yet."

"What do you mean?" Caroline asked.

Marianne stood and walked to the door, then turned around. "Well, maybe you'll decide to get married to Lance after all."

Caroline opened her mouth to dispel Marianne's misconception.

"By the way," Marianne continued. "I saw Lance—I mean, Tru—in the audience. He looked pretty nervous. More nervous than you."

"What?" Caroline gasped.

Marianne winced. "Oh, maybe I shouldn't have said anything. I just assumed you knew he was here."

Caroline forced a smile. "Of course, I knew he was here. I just didn't expect him to come so early, that's all."

Aurora appeared in the doorway and waved over Marianne's shoulder. "They want you in makeup, Dr. Lovelace."

"Well, good luck," Marianne said. "I know you'll be terrific. Ellis is an excellent judge of talent and I'm sure your show will be a big success."

"Thanks," Caroline said.

Marianne turned and smiled at Aurora as she left. Aurora's incredulous gaze followed her out. She turned back to Caroline. "What's gotten into her? Somebody slip her some 'nice' pills?"

Caroline hurried over to the door and dragged Aurora inside. "Never mind her!" she cried. "Tru is in the audience."

Aurora laughed and clapped her hands, then did a little dance around the room. "The Knight of Swords is here? Am I good or what? Didn't I tell you this would happen? Now do you believe?"

Caroline groaned. "All I believe is that I'm about to throw up. You have to go out there and tell him to leave.

I can't do this if he's sitting in the audience. I'll never be able to concentrate."

"He won't leave," Aurora said. "He's the Knight of Swords. He's resolute."

"Well, you're going to have to tell him to get on his horse and go. I can't do the show with him out there."

Aurora linked her arm around Caroline's and tugged her toward the door. "Sure you can. The Three of Cups was in the tenth position."

"Oh, right," Caroline said sarcastically. "How could I possibly be nervous? The Three of Cups. I should have known."

"The tenth position is the final outcome. The Three of Cups is success, good fortune, victory. You have nothing to worry about."

Caroline moaned and fought back a rising panic. For once, she wished that she had more faith in Aurora's powers. Maybe then she wouldn't feel as if she were about to make the biggest blunder of her professional career.

TRU SLOUCHED down into his chair as Caroline walked out on stage and was introduced to the studio audience. She looked tentative and anxious. And vulnerable. He wanted to walk down to the stage and take her in his arms and make all her fears disappear. But he knew he couldn't.

The taping began with a short explanation of the format of the show that Caroline read off the TelePrompter. She seemed to relax a little more as time passed and he watched as Carly Lovelace slowly emerged. The husband she was interviewing appeared on stage first and she prompted him to tell about the problems he perceived in his marriage. The audience, which had been lukewarm at the beginning of the taping, now seemed to be more attentive as she asked probing questions and made illuminating observations.

After fifteen minutes, the husband left the stage and there was a short break in the taping. He kept his eyes focused on Caroline as she stood off to one side. Every now and then, she looked out into the audience, as if she were searching for a familiar face or some indication of how she was doing.

Taping began again once the wife was settled on the stage and fifteen minutes later, her story had been told, with only two stops and starts this time. There was a general hum of anticipation in the audience when the husband joined the wife and the show seemed to take on a more intense atmosphere.

He had to admit, the format for the show was irresistible. He felt a bit guilty, as if he were eavesdropping on someone's private life, watching their relationship fall apart in front of him as they aired their dirty laundry. But as Caroline began to work with the couple he realized that she wasn't tearing them apart, she was putting them back together.

Another twenty-minute segment passed, this time without a miscue, and Tru sat in the darkened studio, unable to take his eyes off of her. She moved with such ease, all her earlier tension and stiffness gone. He could tell she'd forgotten her fears and was focused on what she did best—communicate. She had the audience in the palm of her hand, laughing in one instant and fighting back tears in the other. Ellis had been right about her— she was a natural.

The house lights came up and audience members stood to make their way to the two stationary microphones in the center of each aisle. Her attention was now focused out into the studio, and he slouched down farther in his back row chair. One by one, questions were posed to the couple and answers were given. He found himself standing and joining the line at the microphone. Then suddenly he was next, but he wasn't quite sure what he would say.

"We have time to take one more question from the audience," Caroline said.

"I have a question, Dr. Lovelace," Tru said.

She looked in his direction and her expression froze. "On second thought," she said smoothly, "it looks like we don't have time for another question." She turned back to the couple on the stage.

"Well, then, I don't have a question," Tru replied. "It's more like a hypothetical situation."

"Well, we don't have time for one of those either," Caroline said. "It's time for us to do the close now, sir."

The audience watched their verbal sparring match as if it were a tennis game, their heads bobbing back and forth with each serve and volley. The stage crew and cameramen joined in.

"Let him ask his question!" an audience member cried.

Slowly, she turned back to face him and stepped to the edge of the stage. The cameras followed her and one pointed directly at him. Caroline glanced over at her producer for help, but the woman only shrugged and waved her on. No one seemed overly concerned and Tru suspected that his question would end up on the editing room floor anyway.

The audience slowly melted into the background as their gazes locked. Her expression softened slightly and a reluctant smile touched the corners of her lips. He smiled back. Then he saw it, there, in her glittering green eyes, and he knew he'd made the right choice.

"I used to be married," he began. "I had a wonderful wife. She was everything I ever wanted in a woman. But I made a mistake and she couldn't forgive me and I lost her. I was wondering if you might know how I could make it up to her."

Tru thought his disruption of the show's format would prompt some kind of intervention, but no one moved. It was as if everyone knew there was something important being resolved right in front of them and they weren't about to stop it.

"Does your wife still love you?" Caroline asked softly, her brow arched.

"I think she does," Tru said. "I don't know. What do you think?"

Caroline drew a shaky breath. "I think she was very hurt that you had betrayed her. She had come to trust you and believe in you and you let her down."

"I didn't mean to," Tru said. "I tried to fix the problem before she found out, but that didn't work."

"Maybe if you would have told her the truth, I—*she* would have understood."

He grinned at her and shook his head.

"All right," she agreed. "Maybe not. But you could have at least tried."

"I didn't want to lose her. I loved her. I still do. And I want us to have a future together."

"Do you plan to tell her this?" Caroline said.

"As soon as I can," he replied.

"And do you promise to be honest with her from now on? Do you promise to make an effort to communicate openly?"

"I'd promise to lasso the moon if it would make her happy."

He watched as Caroline blinked back a misty sheen of tears and smiled at him. "I may be able to help you with your problem. Why don't you stick around after the show. I'll give you some free advice."

She turned to the camera on the right side of the stage. "Thank you for joining us today. Be sure to be with us tomorrow on 'Making Your Marriage Work.' For today's couple and our audience, this is Dr. Carly Lovelace reminding you to get back to the basics of love."

With that, the show was over and the audience clapped their hearty approval. The couple on the stage hugged and cried and Caroline went over to say a few words. Tru slowly walked back to his seat, satisfied that he had done what he could. It was now up to her. She'd either come back out to him with her guns blazing or she'd be willing to listen to what he had to say. He watched her disappear backstage and he couldn't help but feel that his whole life was on the line.

Twenty minutes later, the studio was empty and the lights were dimmed. He still sat in his chair, staring down at the stage and watching as the stagehands dismantled the set. He had been tempted to go find her, but he didn't want to spoil her moment of glory, to see anger and mistrust glitter in her happy eyes. A sliver of doubt pierced his heart and he was nearly certain that the delay didn't bode well for his cause.

Footsteps sounded on the stage and echoed through the studio. He glanced down and watched as she wandered out and squinted into the shadows of the seats. She held a huge bouquet of roses in her arms. Slowly, he stood and walked down the aisle to the stage.

"You were incredible," he said. "The show will be a big success. The audience loved you."

She smiled and brushed her cheek against one of the roses. He clenched his hands, imagining the feel of her skin beneath his fingers. "What about you?" she breathed.

"I would have loved you no matter what," he said.

He stepped up on the stage and walked toward her, stopping just inches in front of her. He wanted to pull her into his arms, to draw her body along his until he could feel every sweet curve and delicate bone. Gently, he placed his palm on her cheek. She turned into his touch and closed her eyes.

"I'm sorry, Caroline. I made a mistake. But I promise that I will spend the rest of my life making it up to you. I'll make you happy and I'll love you like no other man can."

He bent and covered her mouth with his in a sweet, lingering kiss. Then he pulled back and looked deep into her eyes. There was love there, and trust, and with that, a future together.

She drew a deep breath and smiled radiantly. "You understand this won't be easy."

He laughed and yanked her into his arms, crushing the roses between them as he spun her around. "Nothing worth having ever is, Dr. Leighton."

\* \* \* \* \*

### COMING UP IN BACHELOR ARMS
*Next month, don't miss* The Strong Silent Type *(March 1995, #529), another delightful book by popular Kate Hoffmann in Temptation's exciting* **Bachelor Arms** *miniseries. Discover how rational*

*and reserved Josh's life changes drastically when he gets roped into the task of taming tabloid darling Taryn Wilde.*

*In April, find out how determined bachelor Garrett McCabe gets an unwanted lesson in domestic bliss from homemaking expert Emily Taylor in* A Happily Unmarried Man *(#533) by Kate Hoffmann.*

*Soon to move into* **Bachelor Arms** *are the heroes and heroines in books by bestselling authors JoAnn Ross, Candace Schuler and Judith Arnold. Don't miss their stories!*

**HARLEQUIN®**

*Temptation.*

*Secret Fantasies*

*Do you have a secret fantasy?*

Reporter Darien Hughes does. While celebrating her thirtieth birthday, she spots a gorgeous man across the crowded restaurant. For fun, she writes about this "secret fantasy man" in her column. But Darien gets a shock when "Sam" shows up at the paper! Enjoy #530 NIGHT GAMES by Janice Kaiser, available in March 1995.

*Everybody* has a secret fantasy. And you'll find them all in Temptation's exciting new yearlong miniseries, Secret Fantasies. Beginning January 1995, one book each month focuses on the hero or heroine's innermost romantic fantasies....

**HARLEQUIN®**

**Deceit, betrayal, murder**

Join Harlequin's intrepid heroines, India Leigh
and Mary Hadfield, as they ferret out the truth
behind the mysterious goings-on in their
neighborhood. These two women are no milk-
and-water misses. In fact, they thrive on

# *MISCHIEF & MAYHEM*

Watch for their incredible adventures in this
special two-book collection. Available in March,
wherever Harlequin books are sold.

On the most romantic day of the year, capture the
thrill of falling in love all over again—with

## Harlequin's

## Bachelors

They're three sexy and *very single* men who run
very special personal ads to find the women of
their fantasies by Valentine's Day. These exciting,
passion-filled stories are written by bestselling
Harlequin authors.

*Your Heart's Desire* by Elise Title
*Mr. Romance* by Pamela Bauer
*Sleepless in St. Louis* by Tiffany White

Be sure not to miss Harlequin's Valentine Bachelors,
available in February wherever
Harlequin books are sold.

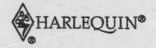

Harlequin invites you to the most
romantic wedding of the season.

Rope the cowboy of your dreams in
**Marry Me, Cowboy!**

A collection of 4 brand-new stories,
celebrating weddings, written by:

*New York Times* bestselling author

# JANET DAILEY

### and favorite authors

## Margaret Way
## Anne McAllister
## Susan Fox

Be sure not to miss Marry Me, Cowboy!
coming this April

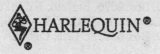 **HARLEQUIN®**

MMC

**HARLEQUIN®** *Temptation*

## BACHELOR ARMS SURVEY

### Vote for Your Favorite!

If all these guys were bachelors, who would you most want to catch? Please! Just choose one from this delectable dozen!

- 1 ☐ Mel Gibson
- 2 ☐ Sean Connery
- 3 ☐ Kevin Costner
- 4 ☐ Alec Baldwin
- 5 ☐ Denzel Washington
- 6 ☐ Tom Cruise
- 7 ☐ Andre Agassi
- 8 ☐ Michael Jordan
- 9 ☐ Jack Nicholson
- 10 ☐ Robert Redford
- 11 ☐ Paul Newman
- 12 ☐ Keanu Reeves

We want to hear from you, so please send in your response to:

In the U.S.: BACHELOR ARMS,
P.O. Box 9076, Buffalo, NY 14269-9076
In Canada: BACHELOR ARMS,
P.O. Box 637, Ft. Erie, ON L2A 5X3

Name: _____

Address _____ City: _____

State/Prov.: _____ Zip/Postal Code: _____

HTBA